This
Time
Around

DIONNE WILSON

Books may be purchased at www.amazon.com

Scripture quotations are taken from the following: The King James Version of the Bible. Public domain.

Publishers Note: This book is a work of fiction. Names, characters, places, and incidents are either products of the author's imagination or used factiously. All characters are fictional, and any similarity to people living or dead is purely coincidental.

Wilson, Dionne
    This Time Around / Dionne Wilson

ISBN 9798586374226
    1. African American Christian – Fiction
    2. Contemporary Women's – Fiction

                Printed in the United States of America

For my sister Terri

CHAPTER ONE

There it was in black and white. And just like that, seven years of marriage, erased in a matter of minutes, Estelle thought as she sat at her dining room table. The hearing, that she did not attend, was said to have lasted a mere fifteen minutes. Fifteen minutes compared to three hours choosing a wedding dress that she wanted to be just right. Fifteen minutes compared to a two-hour church wedding where she walked down the aisle to place her hand in his. Fifteen minutes compared to the countless lunches she packed, meals she prepared, backrubs she gave, the baby they made, but lost. All of those thoughts glided effortlessly through her mind as she looked at the divorce decree in black and white.

The clock read midnight. If she wanted to get any sleep, she needed to go to bed now. Morning would come soon, only to find her tired and restless from a lack of sleep. The alarm would go off with her unready to arise from her bed; her warm, comfortable bed. It still had some converting to memory to do since she had only purchased it a week earlier, but it was becoming the bed she hated to get out of in the morning. It would just be easier to stay there some days. But, her will wouldn't allow her to succumb to that. She had to realize that the worst was behind her.

"Estelle! Estelle!" Jada said, jogging softly to catch up to her colleague and friend. "What do you say to you and me, wearing our tightest dresses and highest heels and going down to the restaurant and bar on Penn Avenue tonight? Some of the finest men go there. And I mean finest men. Chocolate men, caramel men, tall, slender men, short and thick men and a few white men, if that's what you like. Men. Men. Men. Estelle, your divorce is finalized and all these men are available to you. Although they've been available to you."

"Like I've said before, although separated, I was still legally married to him. Dating someone would have been me committing adultery."

"I love you, but I don't get you," Jada said as the two crossed the busy street, "I would have had me about three or four men by now. Yes, one for each season. Love 'em and leave 'em."

A smirk gracing her face, Estelle responded, "You're a mess, but you know that."

"Yes, I do," Jada said. "It is what it is."

"And it ain't what it ain't," Estelle said, bursting into laughter. "You ain't right."

Halting her friend in mid-stride, Jada said, "If loving men is wrong, I don't want to be right. Estelle, I can't be right. My will and my mind won't allow me to be right."

"It's confirmed," Estelle said, pushing Jada's hands from her shoulder all the while attempting to hold in her laughter. "You're like a dude stuck in a woman's body."

"Go ahead and laugh, Estelle," Jada said, gigging hysterically.

"I can't with you. I just can't," Estelle said laughing.

"But, you love me," Jada said, veering left off the walkway. "I don't want to be right. See you at lunch, Estelle."

"Please, upon entering the room, place all papers on the podium," Estelle said as her students made their way into the lecture hall. "Same protocol as the beginning of the semester. If your paper is not on my podium by 9:05, it is considered an incomplete. Not 9:06, 9:07 or beyond. It will not be accepted, unless previously arranged."

"Good morning, Professor Blackwell," a student said, placing his paper on the podium.

"Good morning, Mr. Winters," Estelle said, glancing at her watch. "9:05. I'm glad you made it."

Rushing into the lecture hall, a small delicate hand extended to hurriedly place her paper on the podium.

Snatching the stack of papers off of the podium, Professor Blackwell said, "9:06, Miss Lane, incomplete."

Placing the stack of papers in her satchel, Professor Blackwell returned to the podium.

"Let's begin. We are continuing our lecture on Erikson's theory of psychosocial development. We will begin with the eight stages of psychosocial development, as laid out by Erik Erikson and Joan Erikson. Who would like to begin?"

Looking around the room while leaning on the side of the podium, Professor Blackwell nodded toward Miss Lane. "Miss Lane, perhaps you can redeem yourself and enlighten your fellow classmates by telling us, in your own words, the eight stages, the role they play in social development, if you agree or disagree and why."

"I could just throat punch Precious Lane. She has so much untapped potential, but laziness and mediocrity are standing in her way. She is her own worst enemy and doesn't even know it," Estelle said as she sat across from Jada eating lunch.

"You'll get through to her," Jada said, biting into her Greek feta burger. "I know you will."

"I don't know. This feels tougher than usual," Estelle said, tossing back several sweet potato fries. "I don't know how to get to her. She almost seems unreachable."

"Like I said," Jada said. "You'll figure it out. Now about tonight. I'll meet you there at eight. Is that good for you?"

Estelle nodded reluctantly. "Eight is fine, but don't expect anything out of me. I'm only going because you asked me. I'm not going to meet a man."

"Right," Jada said, taking one last sip of her tea. "You're going to meet many men. One for each year of your life you wasted on that no good ex-husband of yours. I'll see you tonight."

"Bye, Jada," Estelle said as she walked away carrying her tray.

"What to wear?" Estelle spoke out loud as she pushed dresses, rompers and jumpsuits aside in her closet. "None of my clothes are late-night, going-out material." Flopping on the bed in her fluffy, white robe, Estelle thought, "This isn't me." She had never been a part of the night scene. She had no desire for it. She never did, not even in her twenties. It was her ex-husband who enjoyed engaging in the night life. Estelle looked at the clock on her nightstand. It read six o'clock. If she was going to make it in time, she was going to need to get dressed quickly.

Estelle had decided on a basic, black jumpsuit paired with red wedges. She looked herself over in the mirror one last time and decided it was time to head out. "What am I doing? I never do this," she thought, hesitantly grabbing her car keys and walking out the door.

"Hey, Estelle," Jada said excitedly. "I wasn't sure if you were going to make it."

"I wasn't too sure myself," Estelle said, fixing her eyes on the scene before her. Men and women, dressed to the T, looking like they stepped out of a band box, drinks in hands, were milling around engaging in conversation. Some permanent couples and some just-for-the-night couples were dancing together. Others sat and ate elegant meals.

"Everything okay, Estelle?" Jada asked, giving her a puzzled look.

"Yes," Estelle replied with a half smile. "I'm just taking it all in."

"Taking it all in?" Jada asked, confused. "You mean that ex-husband of yours never took you out on a Friday night?"

"No," Estelle said, still observing her surroundings. "He always went out alone, or so I thought."

"And what is it you were doing while he was out alone, or so you thought?"

"I would be sleeping, reading or watching a movie, eating a pizza," Estelle replied, starting to feel uncomfortable. "Look, Jada, I appreciate your intentions, but I should go."

"Don't go," Jada said. "You're here, so at least eat. Dinner is on me."

The place was packed, but it didn't take long getting a table, since Jada had made reservations.

"The food here is amazing," Estelle said, eating her butternut squash ravioli with lobster. "This lobster is delicious."

"And to think, you wanted to leave," Jada said, smiling. "This is my first time ordering the stuffed salmon and I love it!"

"The calamari rings are great, too," Estelle said, picking up another one and taking a bite.

"This is dining at its best," Jada said, eating more of her ravioli. "And you never know who you might run into here, actors, basketball players, football players; Pittsburgh's finest among the professionals."

"I'm not concerned with all of that," Estelle said. "I need to find myself again."

"I say while you're looking for Estelle, find you a man at the same time," Jada said, taking a sip of wine. "You can find a man, or two, or three; starting here tonight."

"My divorce is still fresh," Estelle replied.

"That doesn't make any difference to that ex-husband of yours," Jada said matter of factly. "He's been in and out of relationships during your marriage, through your separation and now. Your divorce being fresh isn't stopping him. Heck, being married to you didn't stop him."

"What my ex-husband did or does is of no concern to me and has no influence over the decisions I make in my life," Estelle stated firmly. "He's my past. I'm the only one responsible for my well-being, a responsibility I handed over too freely in the past. That ended with him."

"I'm sorry, Estelle," Jada said. "This is my way of trying to help. It's the only way I know, love 'em and leave 'em."

The two friends burst into laughter.

"I don't know what I'm going to do with you," Estelle said, smiling.

"You know I'm a keeper," Jada replied.

CHAPTER TWO

Saturday morning arrived sooner than Estelle had anticipated. Not that she had stayed out late with her colleague and friend, however, it was later than usual for her. She enjoyed the food and the overall atmosphere. What she didn't enjoy was the persistent flirting from the men. She had forgotten the pressure on a single woman to grab hold of a guy. On one hand, the flirting showed that she was a beautiful woman, but she already knew that. But, on the other hand it showed how long she had been out of the dating game and she was pretty sure she didn't want to be in it.

Seven a.m. Estelle strapped her cell phone to her arm, pressed play on her playlist, stretched and proceeded to run. She enjoyed her one-mile run each morning. Spring had arrived in Pittsburgh. This is what she longed for all winter when she was forced to run on her treadmill, due to Pittsburgh's brutally cold winters. Being outside in the warm breeze brought life to her.

On her run back toward home, she decided to take a new route. It was a street she rarely took. It had probably been at least a year since her morning run took her this way. Maybe her avoidance had been because of her ex-husband's disdain for the neighborhood and not wanting to purchase their home there. As Estelle made her way past several large, beautiful homes, she came upon the house she adored and had wanted to move into, what seemed like so long ago. There was a moving truck in the driveway. Jogging in place, Estelle paused in front of the house she had longed to call her home. Curious to see who was moving in, without being obvious or creepy, Estelle watched as a man and a woman carried boxes off of the moving truck into the house. The two made an attractive couple. "That should have been my home," Estelle thought as she began to run again.

At that moment, Estelle tripped and fell. Landing on her ankle, Estelle felt a sudden sharp pain shoot upward from her foot to her ankle. Grabbing her ankle, she felt the excruciating pain. Seeing what had happened, as he walked out of his home, the man jogged over to Estelle.

"Is everything okay?" he asked.

"Yes, I'm fine," Estelle said holding her ankle tightly.

"You don't look fine," he said kneeling and gently taking her ankle into his hands.

"Ouch," Estelle cried out in pain, as he pressed lightly on her ankle.

Removing Estelle's shoe, he said, "It's swollen; looks like a bad sprain."

"Yes, I know," Estelle agreed reluctantly. "It's certainly not my first ankle sprain."

"Why don't you stand and see if you can put a little weight on it," he said.

Standing, with assistance from him, Estelle put weight on her injured ankle.

"Oh my God," Estelle cried out. "It hurts so bad."

"Get on my back," he said, kneeling.

Confused, Estelle asked, "What did you say? I don't think I heard you right."

"What you heard is exactly what I said," he answered.

"Do you have any idea how much I weigh?" Estelle asked, still in disbelief at his statement.

Shaking his head while chuckling, he said, "I have a strong back."

Reluctantly, Estelle awkwardly climbed on his back. This is so weird, Estelle thought as he carried her into his house.

"You'll be comfortable here," he said, gently lowering Estelle onto the couch and placing an ottoman under her feet. "You'll want to prop it up at home, above the heart. But, you know that already."

"Can I help you with anything?" a tall, slender woman asked as she entered the living room.

"Yes, some ice please," he said smiling. "Thank you."

Unsure of what to say, besides thank-you, Estelle sat in silence, waiting for the woman to return with the ice. Her ankle was throbbing.

"Here's the ice," the woman said, handing an ice pack and cling wrap to him.

Placing the bag of ice on the side of Estelle's ankle, he secured it by wrapping cling wrap around it.

"Just a little trick I picked up during my high school track days," he said after finishing.

"Do you still run?" Estelle asked.

"When time permits," he said.

"By your response, you must be a busy man," Estelle said, adjusting her seating position on the couch for more comfort.

"Yes, you can say that," he replied, seeming a little embarrassed by her comment.

Returning a smile, Estelle replied, "Okay then. So discreet."

A large smile taking over his face, he replied, "If you must know, I'm an orthopedic surgeon. I just joined the practice working out of Grace Hospital and the Bowman building on Fifth Avenue."

"What do you specialize in?" Estelle asked.

I'm a foot and ankle surgeon," he replied.

"I should have known," Estelle said, smiling.

"Yes," he said. "This can be counted as your first unofficial visit, but I will need to see you on Monday for x-rays. Deal?"

"Deal," Estelle said.

"Rhonda," he called. "Bring me an ankle wrap, 800 mg of ibuprofen and my old crutches."

Entering the room, the woman he referred to as Rhonda handed Estelle the medicine and a glass of water.

"Thank you, Rhonda," Estelle said, taking the medicine and glass of water into her hands.

Handing the ankle wrap to him, Rhonda said, "I'll be back with the crutches."

"You have a beautiful wife," Estelle said.

"Oh, she's all right," he said, laughing while looking at Estelle. "But, she's my sister."

"I heard that," Rhonda said from the hallway.

Removing the ice pack, then slipping the ankle wrap over her ankle, he said, "You'll need to follow the RICE regimen: rest, ice, compression and elevation."

"Thank you," Estelle said. "I really appreciate this."

"No problem," he said, pulling a business card out of his back pocket. "Call first thing Monday morning and tell the front desk that Dr. Alexander said to squeeze you in anytime that's good for you."

"Thank you," Estelle said reading the card, which read, Dr. Kenneth Alexander, Department of Orthopedic Surgery.

"And what is your name so I'll know what name to give the front desk?" Kenneth asked after his sister handed the crutches to him and he adjusted them.

"Dr. Estelle Blackwell."

Smiling, Kenneth said, "A fellow doctor. What is your specialty?"

"I'm a doctor in higher education. I am a tenured professor within the psychology department."

"Impressive," Kenneth said. "Impressive."

Later that afternoon, Estelle relaxed in a warm, bubble bath, thinking about what transpired earlier that morning. Jada will love this, Estelle thought. Her friend would definitely create all kinds of scenarios. Estelle decided not to even try to guess what her friend would say. Estelle would just hear her reaction on Monday.

Pouring herself a cup of chamomile tea, Estelle pulled the hood of her white, plush, hooded robe over her head. It wasn't cold, Estelle simply appreciated the cozy feel of the soft robe. Walking into her living room, she looked through her DVDs, choosing one to watch. Estelle chose a comedy. She needed to laugh. It was in her alone times that thoughts would run rampant in her mind;

thoughts of her broken marriage, the divorce, her husband's infidelity, why she wasn't good enough for her husband, now ex-husband, to love her? Estelle still had a difficult time referring to him as her ex-husband. Unfortunately, these questions crossed her mind way too often. Estelle needed to be free of those thoughts, but when she wasn't busy, her mind ran directly to those thoughts. It picked them apart and dissected them so much, opening the door to a myriad of reasons why she was simply unlovable. Estelle contemplated whether to call her friend Farrah, who was like a sister to her. But, as much as Estelle wanted to call Farrah, who would undoubtedly be there as a listening ear, Estelle knew better. It was time that she faced her thoughts with God as her listener, supporter and comforter. A good friend who is there when you need them most is good. Estelle was sure that no one would believe differently from that. But, there comes a time when everyone must sort out their pain, disappointments and anger with God as their singular listener. Today was that day for Estelle.

Setting her cup of tea on a wooden tray that sat atop the ottoman, Estelle stood, walked out of her living room and up to the master bedroom. She flicked the light switch on in her closet and walked in. Even though it had been awhile, Estelle knew exactly where to find it. Kneeling down on the carpeted floor of her walk-in closet, Estelle moved several shoe boxes aside. After moving the last box, she picked up a medium-sized wooden box. Estelle sat in the middle of her closet, placed the box in front of her and opened it. A journal was inside, filled with written prayers dated one to two years ago. The prayers that filled the pages of her journal were tucked away in a box.

CHAPTER THREE

"I'm disappointed in you, Estelle," Jada said, sipping her latte. "A fine doctor and you didn't invite him to your house."

"Disappointed because I have standards?" Estelle responded as she and her co-worker ate lunch.

"No, I admire you for standards," Jada said. "Lord knows, next to yours, mine are way too low. It's just that I don't understand you at times. You allowed an opportunity to pass you by. You could have at least asked him for his phone number or asked him out on a date. That's all I'm saying."

"Jada, we as women weren't created to pursue men. It's not God's design," Estelle said.

"So, I need to wait on a man to ask me out on a date?" Jada asked.

"Yes, Jada," Estelle answered, taking a sip of water. "He that findeth a wife, findeth a good thing."

"It can say what it wants to say, but for me, if I want to call a man first or ask him out on a date first, that's exactly what I'm going to do," Jada said.

"That's exactly what you're going to do?" Estelle asked, smiling at her co-worker and friend while standing to get her crutches. "You should give being pursued a try. Allow the right man to find you and pursue you, Jada. You're worth it."

Thinking quietly for a moment, Jada looked at Estelle teary-eyed, "Thanks, Estelle, I needed to hear that."

"The good news is that your x-rays don't show any signs of a fracture, as I thought," Dr. Alexander said. "The swelling has gone down significantly. How do you feel?"

"I feel better than I felt on Saturday. I just have a little stiffness," Estelle said, attempting to move her ankle.

"The remedy to the stiffness is for you to move your ankle, even if you feel like you can't," Dr. Alexander said, taking Estelle's ankle into his hands and gently moving it. "I want you to gradually put weight on it over the next few days. When you are able to put all of your weight on it, you can walk without the crutches. I don't expect you to need to use these crutches after the end of this week."

"Sounds good," Estelle said. "When can I get back to running?"

"Here's the deal," Dr. Alexander said. "Come see me again next Monday. If the swelling and pain is completely gone, you can go back to running. Until then no running. Deal?"

"Deal," Estelle said.

"Have a good day, Professor," Dr. Alexander said, smiling as he walked out of the room. "I'll see you next week."

"You say he's a doctor? And he's not married?" Farrah asked as she and Estelle drank lemonade on Estelle's back patio.

"Yes and yes," Estelle said, removing an ice pack from her ankle that she had propped up on a patio chair.

"I'm going to sit back and see how this plays out; see what God has planned," Farrah said.

"See how what plays out?" Estelle exclaimed. "See what God has planned for whom?"

"Don't play dumb, Miss Ph.D.," Farrah said. "I'm going to see what comes of the two of you meeting each other and see what God has planned for you two."

"Nothing is going to come out of us meeting," Estelle said, dipping a tortilla chip into some guacamole. "Absolutely nothing."

"And why not, Estelle?" Farrah asked. "Oh, I forgot, you're Estelle, the unlovable woman."

Looking down at the floor of her patio, Estelle said, "No, because I don't want a repeat of my failed marriage with Clyde."

"Well, do you know how you don't get a repeat?" Farrah asked. "You don't get a repeat by going about dating differently this time around. Your first step to doing things differently is to consult God first on any and every man that wants your time. Also, don't even entertain the thought of spending time with an unsaved man."

"These are things I know," Estelle said quietly.

"I know this, but you didn't follow these principles in the past," Farrah said lovingly. "If you want a better, life-long, loving marriage, then you're going to have to do what you didn't do before. You need a man who holds himself accountable to God, who in turn will hold himself accountable to you."

Later that evening, Estelle enjoyed a nice, quiet dinner alone. It was a beautiful spring day, with the temperature staying in the seventies during the evening, with a nice, light breeze. Estelle decided to enjoy her dinner on the patio. She didn't have anything too heavy or difficult to make. She ate a chicken lettuce wrap and fruit salad along with a tall glass of ice water. Everything is going to be okay, she thought to herself.

CHAPTER FOUR

"Identity versus role confusion; who can tell me the stage and the age range in which it encompasses?" Estelle asked looking out at her students in the lecture hall. "Please everyone, don't volunteer all at once."

Raising her hand, Precious Lane answered, "Identity versus role confusion is the fifth stage of Erikson's psychosocial theory. We experience this stage between the ages of twelve to eighteen."

"And, Miss Lane, what may I ask occurs during this stage?"

"It's where we find ourselves or at least when we should find ourselves. We experiment with different behaviors until we find what fits us best."

"And, Miss Lane, may I ask you what it is that happens if a person does not successfully pass this stage?"

"If we fail this stage, according to Erikson, a strong identity will not be formed, leading to having no direction in life," Precious Lane answered.

"And with that said," Estelle said, looking closely at the class once again. "With no firm foundation of self, one cannot know where they're going in life. Class dismissed. If you have not already done as you should have, the remainder of Erikson's theory needs to be read so that everyone can be an active participant in the discussion."

——

"I cancelled my afternoon classes," Estelle said to Jada as they made their way down the walkway of the university where they taught.

"Where do they do that? Afternoon classes cancelled twice in one week?" Jada asked, looking her co-worker up and down. "I wish I didn't have to grand jete', arabesque or plie' this afternoon. This dancer needs a break. Seriously."

"Then take a break," Estelle said, chuckling. "Don't get an attitude with me."

"I just may do that," Jada said, taking a sip from her water bottle. "You know what, I will."

"Your class will appreciate having an afternoon off," Estelle said. "What do you plan on doing?"

"Going to sleep," Jada said. "I need to relax."

"I need to rest, too," Estelle said. "Let's take a break at this bench. Being injured has worn me out."

Sitting on the bench, Jada thought for a moment and then began to speak. "You know, Estelle, I've thought a lot about our conversations and what you said to me a few days ago. I never really thought about my worth."

"You didn't?" Estelle asked nonjudgmentally.

"No, I didn't. I never thought about how a man should treat me or how I should desire to be treated by one. I wasn't taught that."

"I'm sorry that you weren't taught that, Jada. I wish you would have known your worth long ago," Estelle said empathetically. "But, it's not too late. Today, right now, can be the day."

"I don't know where to begin," Jada said, watching students walk by. "I used to feel so carefree. But, somewhere along the way that changed. I began to care and it frightened me. For the first time in my life I saw my life for what it was."

"And you say it frightened you?" Estelle asked. "Why did it frighten you?"

"Because, here I am, almost forty, and alone," Jada said. "I can't keep friends. I'm surprised you speak to me. I can't keep a man, no matter how hard I try, so I get several to always have one around."

"It sounds to me that you're searching for something, Jada," Estelle said looking at her friend. "What are you searching for?"

Tears streaming down her face, Jada said, "I'm searching for me."

Placing the wooden box on her dresser, Estelle took her journal and an ink pen out of the box and wrote Jada's name in her journal. Estelle added the date and placed the journal with her friend's name in it back in the box.

Rummaging through her fridge, Estelle realized her dire need to go grocery shopping. Not finding anything that she desired to eat, she decided to order a pizza. Pizza and a movie it would be for her night, she thought to herself. Estelle wasn't halfway through the movie when she fell asleep. When she woke up, the clock read three a.m. Feeling rejuvenated, Estelle was sure that she would not be able to go back to sleep. Adjusting her eyes, Estelle saw the wooden box sitting on top of her dresser. She decided to pray. Estelle walked to the dresser and picked up the box. She hopped back onto her bed. Opening the box and removing the journal, Estelle looked through her old prayers. The first name she read was Clyde, her ex-husband. It was dated last year. Estelle had prayed for him and their marriage, even when they were separated. She wrote an uppercase U next to Clyde's name indicating that was an unanswered prayer. Other prayers were for God's peace, healing after her miscarriage, a new home and one for her friend Farrah to be healed from cancer, to name a few. She still desired a new home, so Estelle made a new list for things she still needed to pray about. Among that list were prayers for her friend Jada and she added two new prayers, one for God's direction and another for God's forgiveness.

CHAPTER FIVE

Sunday morning. Oh, how Estelle loved Sunday mornings. It was a day of rejuvenation for her. Putting on her pink, freshwater pearl necklace and earrings, Estelle looked herself over one last time in her full-length mirror in her bedroom. She looked better than she felt. She couldn't sleep last night because of all the pain that filled her heart. Although it was old pain, her wounds were deep-rooted. Estelle hated that Clyde could hold so much power over her life. The ongoing relationship between him and his ex-girlfriend that was never severed between the two, even when she and Clyde took their wedding vows, had hurt Estelle deeply. Estelle still couldn't understand what kind of man would marry a woman, only to continue a physical relationship with his ex-girlfriend. Estelle had recently heard from a mutual acquaintance that Clyde and his ex, turned mistress, had had a baby together. Their baby had been conceived while Clyde and Estelle were still married. The sting of Clyde's betrayal and deception was as fresh as the day Estelle discovered Clyde's infidelity. Estelle wasn't bitter. As a result of Clyde's infidelity and deceit, she now didn't hate or mistrust all men. In fact, Estelle didn't even hate Clyde. She simply felt a plethora of emotions for being a substitute until a woman from Clyde's past decided to give their relationship a second chance, all at the expense of Estelle's heart and marriage. It was a deep jab to her spirit.

Praise and worship proved to be a press, as Estelle's spirit lamented Clyde's infidelity and the baby he conceived with his mistress. "God, why did my baby have to die," Estelle thought, almost seemingly audibly. "Why didn't my husband love me or our unborn child?" Estelle had to push those thoughts, which grew negative emotions, out of her mind to enter into the realm of worship. Estelle was the worship leader at the Baptist church on Flynn Avenue in Homestead. She had to put everything aside and allow herself to be used by God.

"Lord, I lift," Estelle sang in her strong, spirit-filled, anointed, alto voice. "How I love, love…"

"How I love to sing your praises," the praise team and congregation sang in the background.

"I'm so glad, glad, glad," Estelle sang boisterously, tapping her hand against her leg.

"I'm so glad you came to save us," the praise team and congregation followed.

As the service moved on, Estelle found herself more engrossed in praise and worship. Although her situation hadn't changed, her sacrifice of praise unto God, made the pain in her heart feel lighter.

"You deserve it," Estelle proclaimed, hands lifted, tears running down her face. "Oh, Lord, you deserve my praise. No matter what I'm going through, you deserve it. Oh, Lord, your Son Jesus gave His life for me. He didn't have to do it, but He did it just for me. And, Lord, I'm grateful."

"It's a beautiful day for a stroll," Farrah said. "How about a walk around the Lakefront?"

"Sounds good to me," Estelle said. "Then we can grab something to eat."

"That sounds good. Let me just find Lewis to let him know where I'm going."

Lewis was Farrah's husband of five years. Farrah and Lewis were married shortly after Estelle and Clyde. One major difference in the marriages was that Lewis was faithful to Farrah and Clyde had not been faithful to Estelle.

"Ready?" Farrah asked, walking back toward Estelle.

"Ready," Estelle answered.

"The weather outside today is so nice," Farrah said, as the two friends walked along the sidewalk passing shops and others enjoying the lovely Sunday afternoon. "This is the weather I've been waiting for."

"Me, too," Estelle said. "I love warm weather, especially because I get to break out my sandals, sundresses and sun hats. Need I say more?"

"I believe you covered it all," Farrah said as the two friends turned to walk over a bridge that overlooked traffic below. "You sure sang this morning. The spirit of God flowed through you effortlessly."

Stopping on the bridge to view the cars riding beneath them, Estelle said, "I'm glad it appeared effortless. At first it wasn't. It was a press; a tough one."

"You definitely gave your sacrifice of praise," Farrah said, leaning her back on the rail of the bridge, her eyes filling with tears. "You definitely blessed me."

Placing her hand on her friend's shoulder, Estelle asked, "Is everything all right with you, Farrah?"

Shaking her head back and forth, more tears streaming down her face, Farrah said, "I don't know how to say it."

"The thing is, Farrah, just like I tell the students I counsel, you don't need to choose elegant words or the right words; you just say it."

Wiping her tears and looking her friend in the eye, Farrah said, "I found another lump. I was taking a shower one morning, decided to do my breast self-examination and I found another lump."

Staying quiet for a moment, Estelle searched for the right words to say. Although, as a counselor, she encouraged others to just say it, she knew that her words always had to be chosen carefully. As a counselor, with others seeking help from her, her words held the power to shape someone's perspective, possibly making a bad situation worse. Estelle spoke, "Farrah, with all that you've been through with having breast cancer in the past, I can fully empathize with your fear. No one wants to survive cancer only to be faced with the possibility of having to fight that battle again. However, without a diagnosis of cancer, you've got to look at this for what it is, a scare. But, Farrah, don't give into the fear. Don't allow your joy to be taken away by the fear of the unknown. Have you scheduled an appointment with your doctor?"

"Yes, I did," Farrah answered through sniffles.

"Good," Estelle said. "My advice is to not worry. I'm believing that when God healed you the first time that His healing was final."

"I don't know what to think, Estelle."

"Don't think," Estelle said, placing her hand upon her friend's hand. "Just trust."

CHAPTER SIX

The spring semester was coming to an end. Summer was near. Estelle was looking forward to the break. Multiple vacations awaited her. Soon she would find herself enjoying time on Lake Erie. Mid-summer would find her taking in the majesty of Niagara Falls. She would end her summer spending a weekend in a cabin with Jada and Farrah.

Jada and Farrah, Estelle thought to herself. Her two friends were facing some tough issues. Doctoring a migraine, Estelle decided to cancel classes for the day, which was something Estelle rarely did. But, her headache this particular morning was excruciating. It was quite cool in her home, so Estelle put a caftan on to knock the chill of the morning from her body. Estelle wondered if she was getting sick after looking at the thermostat, which read seventy degrees. Already past the bathroom, Estelle was trying to decide if she would continue toward the stairs or turn back to get the thermometer. She decided to continue toward the stairs. There was also a thermometer in the cabinet of the first-floor bathroom.

With the world full of technology, state- of-the-art appliances and gadgets, Estelle still enjoyed the whistle of an old-fashioned teapot. It was comforting in a nostalgic kind of way. The teapot Estelle used had belonged to her late grandmother, Mama Odella. She had fond memories of visiting Mama Odella, as she was lovingly called by all of her grandchildren. Mama Odella's kitchen was always brewing tea; chamomile, green tea, black tea, white tea.

Mama Odella was a firm believer of the healing powers held within a cup of tea. If a woman needed to lose weight or lower her cholesterol, Mama Odella would treat her to white tea. Black tea would be recommended to all the workers working the graveyard shift to keep them awake, alert and energized. And for an upset stomach, Estelle's favorite, chamomile tea, which she would enjoy this morning. Although she didn't have an upset stomach, a nice cup of chamomile tea, followed by a warm bath and a nap, always took a migraine away. But, what relieved her migraines better than any of those things was when Mama Odella would massage her temples and scalp. Estelle would fall asleep next to her grandmother, as she would gently massage her scalp, relieving all of the pain. The healing touch of her grandmother helped her every time. How Estelle longed for Mama Odella now, for more reasons than one.

Later that afternoon, Estelle received a text from Jada:

Missed you today. Hope you're feeling better. I'll stop by this evening to check on you.

Jada, Estelle thought to herself, talented, smart, caring, giving, fun and loving, yet she didn't see her worth. How could someone with all of her degrees, talent, accolades and beauty think that she wasn't worth loving? Why did Jada interact with men the way that she did?

Setting her cell on her nightstand, Estelle rolled over and fell back to sleep.

"Estelle! Estelle!"

Awakening from her nap, Estelle was startled by Jada's voice coming from the direction of the back patio. Estelle looked out her bedroom window and sure enough there stood Jada with a take-out bag in her hand.

"Come open this door, Estelle!" Jada hollered when she saw Estelle look out the window.

Glancing at her alarm clock, Estelle saw that it read six o' clock p.m. Wow, she had slept a long time, she thought to herself. But, at least her migraine was gone.

"Oh, my goodness," Jada said when Estelle opened the patio door to let her into the kitchen. "I've been calling your cell, texting you and hollering outside your window for the last twenty minutes. I almost took my food and went home."

"You weren't going anywhere," Estelle said. "Sit down. What's in the bag?"

Taking a seat at the kitchen table, Jada responded sarcastically, "Can't you read?"

"Girl, give me my sandwich," Estelle said sitting next to her friend. "Turkey?"

"Yes, with mayo and a little lettuce," Jada said, tossing Estelle a bag of kettle chips. "Here's your bag of chips, heifer."

"The treatment I get," Estelle said jokingly. "The names I'm called."

"Exactly," Jada said smiling. "You get treatment from a caring friend who brings food to you."

"Thank you," Estelle said before biting into her Jim John's sandwich, "So fresh."

"It looks like you're feeling better."

"I am," Estelle said. "Much better."

"That's good."

"How are you feeling?"

"Are you referring to how I am feeling since our talk?"

"Yes," Estelle said.

"I have my good days and some bad days," Jada said.

"And that's okay," Estelle said looking at her friend. "Right?"

"I'm not going to lie. I don't know, Estelle."

"And it's totally okay not to know," Estelle said looking out the window at the trees that surrounded her backyard. "That's where so many people get caught up, thinking they have to know. God doesn't require us to know if everything is going to be all right, He requires us to have faith that everything will be all right."

"Faith," Jada said. "That's something I sure don't have."

"Faith comes through knowing God, Jada," Estelle said. "And we only know God through His Son Jesus Christ."

"Jesus Christ," Jada said, teary-eyed. "What would He want to do with me? I'm a mess."

"Jada, we're all a mess, but Jesus loves us through our mess. He cleanses our mess," Estelle said. "That's what the cross is about, the day an innocent man took our sins as His own to make our relationship right with God."

"God loves me even with all the men I've been with?"

"Yes, Jada, He does."

"I've been with many men, Estelle."

"It doesn't matter," Estelle spoke softly.

"I feel too dirty to be loved by God."

"We all are dirty before Jesus cleanses us. Even me."

Wiping a tear from her face, Jada asked, "How do I become clean? What do I need to do?"

Leaning close to her friend and taking her hand into hers, Estelle spoke softly, "It's not what you need to do, Jada, it's what you need to believe. Nothing we can do can make us clean. We must have faith and believe we are clean."

"Have faith and believe?"

"Yes, have faith, confess with your mouth and believe in your heart that Jesus died for you. Ask Him to come into your heart to transform you."

"Is that all?"

"You must also admit that you are a sinner, ask for forgiveness and you shall be saved."

"Estelle, I want to be saved."

Hugging Jada, Estelle said, "I'm so happy for you, Jada. God loves you so much. I've been praying for this day."

"You have?"

"Yes, I have," Estelle said, still holding her friend's hands. "Repeat after me."

CHAPTER SEVEN

The spring semester had finally come to an end. Estelle was thankful for that. Placing items that she wouldn't need for the next school term into a medium-sized box, Estelle heard a light knock on her office door.

"Come in, it's open," Estelle said, setting the box on an ottoman that sat in a corner of her office.

"Professor Blackwell," one of Estelle's students spoke. "I'm glad I didn't miss you."

"Miss Lane," Estelle said. "What brings you by today?"

Stepping closer to Estelle's desk, which separated the two, Precious Lane spoke. "Professor Blackwell, I just wanted to thank you."

"You're welcome, Miss Lane, but can I ask what you are thanking me for?"

"For challenging me to do better, to be better," Precious Lane said. "For pulling out of me what I failed to see in myself."

"Miss Lane, I know greatness when I see it. I've been teaching long enough to know who has it and who doesn't. And you Miss Lane, you have it. Your mind amazes me."

"Thank you," Precious said, turning to leave Estelle's office.

"Before you go, Miss Lane, what grade did you get in my class?"

"An A, Professor Blackwell. You gave me an A."

"Now that's where you're wrong, Miss Lane. I didn't give you an A, you earned an A. I expect the same out of you next year, even with new professors. There's no turning back now, Miss Lane. From this point on, your only option is greatness."

"Enjoy your summer, Professor Blackwell."

"You too, Miss Lane. Stop by next year. My office door will always be open to you."

CHAPTER EIGHT

In the spring and summer months Estelle always did her jogging in the early morning. This day was like any other day. The neighbor three houses down was walking her dog. The older couple next door were enjoying their morning coffee. There were several other joggers in the neighborhood. Estelle inhaled the air and set off to enjoy her beginning of summer.

Rounding a corner, Estelle neared Dr. Kenneth Alexander's home. That man was so handsome, she thought to herself. Single, too. And a doctor. That surely was a perk. Estelle often found herself thinking about Dr. Alexander. Estelle jogged past his home, careful not to stare, just taking a quick glance. It was a Saturday, so the doctor wasn't at work and most likely was at home.

The warm water trickled down Estelle's back. The shower after her jog was always relaxing. The remainder of Estelle's day would be filled with a trip to the grocery store, paying a few bills online, mowing the lawn and having Farrah over for dinner. Although Farrah and Estelle attended the same church, it had been a few weeks since the two friends had some time to themselves to talk. Estelle was looking forward to seeing Farrah.

Rechecking her grocery list confirmed that Estelle had everything on her list inside of her cart.

"Professor Blackwell," a voice spoke gently, placing a hand on Estelle's shoulder.

Turning around, expecting to see a student, Estelle faced Dr. Alexander looking back at her.

"I thought that was you," Kenneth said smiling, showing satisfaction. "How is that ankle of yours? How are you?"

"Well," Estelle answered.

"I can tell," Kenneth said, pleased with what he saw. "You look good, Professor Blackwell."

"Thank you. You look good yourself, Dr. Alexander," Estelle said, blushing. She hadn't flirted or been flirted with in years.

"Are you teaching this summer?"

"No, I get the summer all to myself."

"What are your plans?" Kenneth asked.

"A few getaways, some home projects, pampering."

"Sounds good. What are your plans for this weekend?"

"Pizza and a movie in bed," Estelle said, smiling.

"Is that Saturday or Sunday, Professor Blackwell?"

"That's Friday night," Estelle answered, chuckling.

With a smile on his face Kenneth asked, "Would you like to join me for lunch this Saturday?"

"Yes," Estelle spoke softly, trying to hide her grin. "Yes, I would like to."

"I'm glad," Kenneth said, smiling at Estelle. "What do you say to joining me at Bentley Plaza at noon on Saturday?"

"That sounds good," Estelle said, noticing the gray growing in at Dr. Alexander's temples. So distinguished, Estelle thought. "Should I bring anything?"

"Only your beautiful self," Kenneth answered, looking into Estelle's eyes.

"No he didn't," Farrah said before taking a gulp of ice water.

"Yes, he did," Estelle said, chuckling. "And so confidently. So sure of himself."

"Yes, honey, he just knew you were going to say yes to his invitation," Farrah said between crunching vegetables. "Estelle done went to the grocery store and left with a date."

"Whatever, Farrah," Estelle said, smiling.

"Don't whatever me," Farrah said. "And remember, if you want different results you must do things differently this time around. Remember not to mention anything about your spiritual beliefs. This way it is less likely that he can put on an act; acting like he is saved, sanctified, holy ghost filled, fire baptized."

Bursting into laughter, Estelle asked, "All that, Farrah?"

Leaning forward in the patio chair, Farrah tried to quelch a giggle as she said, "Yes, all that, Estelle. Lest we forget, Mr. Saved, Sanctified Clyde, to me to live is Christ. The moment he found out you were a Christian, he ran with it."

"He did exactly that," Estelle said, shaking her head.

"But, in all seriousness," Farrah said looking at her friend. "Listen carefully to what he says, how he says it, what he chooses to speak about. Leave some mystery to yourself. Don't reveal all of your character traits, whether a strength or a weakness. Don't let him know everything you are on a first date. I don't want to see you manipulated ever again."

"I know. Thank you," Estelle said nervously. "I can't relive a life with Clyde, only with a different name and face."

"No, you definitely cannot."

"You seem like you're in a good place today," Estelle said, taking a bite of her burger she had cooked on the grill.

"I am," Farrah said calmly. "I gave it to God. No fear here. By His stripes I am healed."

CHAPTER NINE

Summer days weren't called the lazy days of summer for no reason. Estelle definitely had been feeling lazy today and the days that had passed. Her only commitment for the day was choir rehearsal and that wasn't until later in the evening. She had hours of free time on her hands. Leaning on the island in her kitchen, Estelle scrolled through her contacts. She paused at Kenneth's name. The fine doctor himself had given her his phone number the day he saw her in the grocery store; in case she would need to cancel their plans for Saturday, which she definitely didn't plan on doing. Estelle thought about giving him a call, just to say hello. But, she then heard Farrah's voice, *"if you want different results, you have to do things differently this time around."* Estelle then remembered her own words of wisdom to Jada, "we as women were not created to pursue men. It's not God's design," Estelle spoke out loud to herself, setting her phone down on the island.

Just as she turned to walk to the refrigerator for a bottle of water, Estelle's phone rang. Stopping mid-stride, Estelle silently lipped his name, "Clyde."

Estelle now realized that she had failed to remove Clyde's name from her contact list. She had recognized his ringtone.

Hesitantly picking up her phone, Estelle answered the call and said, "Hello."

Staring at her bedroom ceiling, Estelle didn't know what to make of Clyde's call or his reason for calling. "I miss you," were his exact words. Yet, Clyde was still in a relationship with his ex-girlfriend turned mistress turned current girlfriend and mother of their child. Estelle couldn't believe his audacity in calling her. It irritated her to her core.

Trying to put Clyde's call out of her mind, Estelle decided to pray. She prayed for Farrah. She thanked God for Jada giving her life to Christ. Estelle prayed for Precious Lane, that she would continue on the road to success. Estelle prayed for herself. She prayed for direction and discernment from God. She prayed for God's forgiveness for marrying Clyde, a man she was never told by God to marry. Estelle felt an uneasiness within, unsure of her ability to reject Clyde's attempt to somehow win her back. In no way did Estelle ever want to be in a relationship with Clyde again. But, would her underlying love for him draw her back?

CHAPTER TEN

Saturday had arrived. Estelle was both excited and nervous at the same time. It had been years since she had been on a date. And even then she hadn't been taken on many dates. Before dating and then marrying Clyde, Estelle had only dated two other men, both very short-lived relationships. What would she talk about without revealing too much? What were the doctor's expectations of her? If it fizzled, how would she feel bumping into him on her morning run or at the grocery store? Was Kenneth Alexander a Christian? She had so many questions running through her mind when she took a quick look at the time. It was time to go if she didn't want to be late. As she began to leave her bedroom, a voice within her whispered the word pray. Estelle stopped in her tracks and prayed.

As she made her way toward the lush, green lawn, the park was a bustle of families and children riding the carousel, friends sharing a meal at one of the kiosks, college students throwing a football. The atmosphere helped Estelle feel relaxed. She was glad of that. After praying, her nervousness began to dissipate. Nearing the lawn, Estelle set her eyes upon Dr. Alexander standing next to a white picnic blanket on the lawn. Upon it lay a wicker picnic basket. Dr. Alexander was dressed in a casual button-up shirt, topped with a bowtie. He wore navy blue oxfords on his feet. He was handsome and well put together from head to toe. It was refreshing to see a man care about his physical appearance, yet not be full of himself.

When Kenneth noticed Estelle approaching, he confidently walked toward her.

"Hello, Estelle," Kenneth said, a gentle smile on his face. "You look beautiful."

"Thank you," Estelle said, as he gently took her hand into his, leading her to the picnic blanket he had set up.

"Today turned out to be a nice day," Kenneth said. "Not too hot, but just right."

"Yes, the weather is just right," Estelle replied, not knowing what to say next.

Opening the picnic basket, Kenneth removed a cold salad and fried chicken.

"I didn't think I could go wrong with pasta salad and chicken. Did I?" Kenneth asked as he set out two plates.

"No, no you didn't," Estelle answered as he served her and then himself.

After putting food on each of their plates, Kenneth stretched his hands toward Estelle and said, "Let us pray."

After praying, Kenneth removed a bottle of sparkling water and poured a cup for each of them.

"Thank you," Estelle said. "This is lovely."

"You're welcome. It's my pleasure."

The afternoon proved to be relaxing and enjoyable. Dr. Alexander shared with Estelle his pastime of playing basketball, although he had never played in high school or college. Although relocating to Pittsburgh, he and Estelle did not root for the same football team. Estelle shared with him the details of the memoir she was currently reading, in which Kenneth showed genuine interest. The two spoke about music, even throwing in a few dance moves from the '90's, causing great laughter.

"Would you like a slice of cake?" Kenneth asked, removing a lid from a container that held two slices of pound cake.

"Yes, I would," Estelle replied. "The meal was delicious and I know the cake will be, too."

"I'm happy that you enjoyed it. I'm enjoying my time with you," Kenneth said. "And I believe it is safe to say that you are enjoying your time with me, too."

"Yes, I am," Estelle said as their eyes met.

He has honest eyes, Estelle thought to herself.

"It's been some time since I've courted a beautiful woman," Dr. Alexander said, grinning. "I didn't know how I would do."

"You did well," Estelle said, smiling at the doctor. "I'm impressed."

"Thank you, but you, Estelle Blackwell, are impressive to me. You're beautiful on the inside and out. You're intelligent and can hold a conversation. I like that in a woman, beauty and brains. You, Estelle, are refreshingly beautiful."

"Thank you, Kenneth."

"Girl, he did not say you're refreshingly beautiful," Farrah said. "You better keep him."

Smiling while placing her friend on speakerphone, even though Farrah hated it, Estelle said, "Farrah, a keeper after one date?"

"Estelle, I know when a man is a keeper and Kenneth Alexander is a keeper. Just you wait and see."

"I will wait and see," Estelle said, removing her flowy tank top and bra, replacing it with a sports bra then lying down on her bed.

"Am I on speaker?" Farrah asked.

"You've been on speaker," Estelle said, removing her friend from speakerphone. "As if anyone else is here. It's just you, me and JC and He can hear you on or off speakerphone."

"JC? Oh, yeah, JC as in Jesus Christ. You're right about that," Farrah said. "I got a good report at my doctor's appointment. The lump I found was nothing."

"I'm so glad," Estelle said. "I have been claiming you were completely healed."

"I thank you, Estelle. God has truly blessed our friendship," Farrah said.

"Yes, He has," Estelle agreed.

"Now tell me more about your date with the doctor."

CHAPTER ELEVEN

A few months had passed since Estelle and Kenneth's first date. A few months had also passed since Estelle's unexpected call from Clyde. Clyde had proven to be persistent in his pursuit of her. He had called several times within the last few months. He was adamantly pursuing Estelle and she didn't quite understand why. She couldn't figure it out and she definitely didn't like it. She didn't like it at all.

It was July. Estelle had already spent her mini-vacation relaxing at Presque Isle. She was now enjoying the beauty of Niagara Falls. Estelle had decided to have Jada join her to keep her company, instead of going alone, as previously planned.

"I don't like it. I don't like it one bit," Jada said, sprawling out on one of the full-sized beds after she and Estelle enjoyed an afternoon admiring the falls. "He's lowdown and he's no good."

"He mentioned to me something along the line of no longer living with his girlfriend."

"And that's your concern?" Jada asked. "I hope ol' dude doesn't think he's moving in with you. Please don't tell me he asked you."

"No, he didn't ask me," Estelle said flinging her sun hat on the other bed and flopping down in a nearby seat.

"Good," Jada replied.

"At least not directly," Estelle added.

"At least not directly?" Jada asked confused, popping up to a sitting position.

"Yes, at least not directly," Estelle said, breathing deeply. "Clyde keeps asking questions about the spare bedroom, asking if I turned it into a reading room or a gym. When we were married I never could decide. When I answered that it was still set up as a guest room, he said something about all that room in that house going to waste."

"If he really thinks you would allow him to move in with you, then that man is dumber than I thought."

"I don't know what he's thinking," Estelle said, staring out the floor-to-ceiling length window at the beautiful city of Toronto. "But, what I do know is that he is desperate."

"Among other things," Jada said.

"Well, no matter what he is, all he is getting from me is prayer," Estelle said pulling the curtains shut and turning to her friend. "Enough about Clyde. I don't know about you, but there's more of the city I want to see."

CHAPTER TWELVE

"You seem a little preoccupied," Kenneth said, looking at Estelle across the table. "A little agitated, maybe? Did I say something to make you upset?"

"No, Kenneth," Estelle said, gently placing her hand over his. "I am a bit agitated, but it's not by you."

Kenneth and Estelle had been enjoying spending time with each other. It was nearing the start of the fall semester. The relaxing days of summer caused Estelle to not want summer to end. But, summer would be ending soon. At least her time spent with Kenneth would go on. Sitting in the open-air restaurant in the Heritage District, Estelle thanked God for the time she had during her separation with Clyde. The time leading up to the divorce gave her time to reconnect with God, set some things straight and begin to put God first again in her life. Yes, she cared for Kenneth, but her love for God would always be greater. God was first in Estelle's life, as well as in Kenneth's life, which Estelle came to know early on in their relationship. That was why she continued to spend time with him.

"Would you like to share with me what is bothering you?" Kenneth asked.

"Thanks, but I'll be fine," Estelle said. "I'm not going to ruin our evening."

"Nothing could ruin our evening. I really enjoy spending time with you, Estelle," Kenneth said. "But, whatever is bothering you I pray that God removes it. It's a battle, Estelle. It's a battle for your heart. I don't know what or who it is, but something or someone is trying to steal your peace, your joy. But, what I do know is that it won't win. It can't win. It's about to end soon. Seek God and He'll lead you."

That's what Estelle liked most about Kenneth. He was so connected to God. Second to admiring his relationship with God through Christ, Estelle enjoyed looking upon his handsome face.

"You're telling me the doctor knew and spoke exactly to your situation and you never told him about Clyde contacting you?"

"Yes, he did and no, I never told Kenneth about Clyde contacting me." Estelle said."

"Just more confirmation that he is a keeper," Farrah said.

Smiling, Estelle said, "I knew you would say that."

"You know me too well," Farrah said, smiling.

"Yes, I do," Estelle said. "Farrah, I'm so mentally tired of dealing with Clyde."

"I know," Farrah said softly. "God knows, too. So, enough talking to me. Go talk to God."

Hanging up the phone, Estelle sat on her bed to begin to pray. But, then Estelle recalled a sermon preached by one of the ministers at church, in which she said, sometimes we have to change positions; physical positions when praying to God. She spoke of going to the threshing floor. Estelle looked up at the ceiling and with tears in her eyes she then laid prostrate on the floor. Estelle prayed out loud to God and she could feel His presence there.

CHAPTER THIRTEEN

Estelle still couldn't believe what she was about to do. However, with God's leading she was going to go through with it. It was a bold move on her part, a move she would never make if she didn't feel the nudging of the Holy Spirit.

Estelle walked confidently into the coffee shop. Glancing around the small, intimate space, she didn't see him sitting at any of the tables. She would order a latte and a pastry and wait.

Taking the last sip of her latte, Estelle looked up to see him walking toward her table. No turning back now, she thought. God, I hope that I heard you correctly, she also thought.

"Estelle," he said, standing beside the table where she sat.

"Clyde," Estelle spoke, gesturing to the seat across from her. "Please, have a seat."

"I see you ordered your favorite," Clyde said. "You always loved lattes."

Skipping all formalities and small talk, Estelle said, "Clyde, I asked you to meet me here today for one reason and one reason only."

Smiling, Clyde said, "For one reason and one reason only."

Not amused by his assumption, Estelle spoke calmly. "I asked you to meet me here today to tell you to never contact me ever again."

A mixture of confusion and amusement took over Clyde's demeanor as he spoke. "You asked me to meet you here to tell me not to contact you ever again? That's something you could have told me over the phone. Are you sure you didn't ask me to meet you here because deep down inside you wanted to see me again? Come on, Estelle, we're both adults. You can tell me the truth."

"No, Clyde, that is not the reason," Estelle said confidently. "As I said, I asked you to meet me here to tell you face-to-face not to contact me ever again. It is easier for you to see how serious I am face-to-face as opposed to telling you over the phone."

Trying to conceal his anger, Clyde said, "Okay, Estelle, I won't contact you ever again. But, let me ask you a question. Don't you ever get lonely, Estelle? What do you do when you're lonely, Estelle?"

Collecting her belongings from the table, Estelle stood to leave, "I said what I needed to say. I am going to go now. Goodbye, Clyde."

As Estelle walked out of the coffee shop, she felt a peaceful feeling overtake her.

"Why didn't you just get your number changed?" Jada asked.

"God wanted me to handle it a different way. The way I handled it is exactly the way God told me to handle it," Estelle said as the two friends sat side-by-side getting manicures.

"Estelle, I need to be more like you," Jada said.

"Actually, you don't. We all need to be more like Jesus. Me following what God told me to do was exactly like Jesus not saying or doing anything unless it was from His Father, God. Jada, keep seeking God and you will be more and more like Him."

"Do you think Clyde is going to continue to contact you?"

"No, I don't," Estelle said.

"Good," Jada said. "He's your past. You have so much going for you in your present, you don't need him taking your peace."

"You're right about that. I'm in a good place right now; a better place spiritually and emotionally than I've been in over the past couple of years," Estelle said. "I like this place."

CHAPTER FOURTEEN

Sunday morning, the day to enter the house of the Lord to worship. Thinking back over her life, Estelle acknowledged the power of worship. It was her God-given way to war against the enemy and his attempts to steal, kill or destroy God's promises for her life. The attempts never prospered and never would. God was great in her life and greater than any tactics of the enemy.

"Thank you, God, for this day," Estelle spoke out loud. "I praise you, Lord, for your many blessings. You have been gracious and merciful to me. Greater is He that is in me than he that is in the world. Your word tells me that I am more than a conqueror through Jesus Christ. Worship isn't what I do. Worship is my lifestyle, Lord. Thank you, God, I love you."

Giving one last glance at her outfit, Estelle picked up her Bible and walked out of her bedroom.

"This is the day the Lord has made! Let's rejoice!" Estelle spoke vibrantly as the pianist and drummer began to play an upbeat song.

With hands clapping, heads swaying, and voices raised, the congregation cried out, "Rejoice! Hallelujah! Let Jesus be exalted! Magnify the Lord!"

Estelle felt the worship in her soul as she sang, "I was made to worship! You were made to worship! We were made to worship! Let's worship the Lord! Everybody say…"

"I was made to worship! You were made to worship! We were made to worship! Let's worship the Lord!" The praise team and congregation sang with spirit.

"Not gonna let the rocks cry out for me! I will worship the Lord excitedly!" Estelle sang, rocking side-to-side in the pulpit. "Sing it again! Not gonna let the rocks cry out for me. I will worship the Lord excitedly! You say!"

"Not gonna let the rocks cry out for me! I will worship the Lord excitedly!"

"I was created to worship the Lord!" Estelle sang out exuberantly, bringing the song to an end.

Taking her usual seat in the third pew, Estelle observed around her that there were a handful of visitors there today. She wondered if each one was a member at another local church or if they were looking for a church home and God had led them here. Removing an envelope that sat in a holder on the back of the pew, Estelle prepared her tithes and offerings, writing her name on her envelope, placing her money inside and then sealing it. She put her ink pen back in her purse and tucked her tithe envelope in the outside pocket. She sat back and listened to the announcements that were also in the church bulletin. She read along silently as one of the women of the church read them aloud.

"It's summer ladies and do you know what that means! It's time for our first summer women's retreat! Yes, it's retreat time. Time to rejuvenate. Time to refresh. Time to relax. Time to reconnect with God! We still have a few slots left if you ladies know of anyone who would like to attend. See me and as long as you are signed up and paid in full by the end of this month, you can join us. You don't want to miss it."

Walking to the pulpit next was the Sunday school superintendent.

"Good morning. I'm here on behalf of the Sunday school. We are hosting a teen forum that will take place in August. We will focus on social issues that teens face and the role of spirituality in those issues. We are in the process of finalizing the speaker panel and need suggestions for Christian school counselors, therapists and doctors. We're looking for Christian professionals who can give a clear Biblical response to issues teens face on a daily basis. You can contact me or one of the Sunday school teachers for any suggestions you may have. Thank you."

The next person to step behind the pulpit was one of the several ministers of the church who was officiating service.

"We know that God is a healer. We must confess that we're not going to be healed, but we're already healed. When Jesus gave His life on the cross, He not only took our sins, but He healed us of our infirmities as well.

It's praying time, saints. By His stripes we are healed. But we must have faith. If we come before God, we must come with a believing heart. We must make up in our minds, that no matter what it looks like, no matter what it feels like, we shall believe the report of the Lord. Say with me, saints, I'm not moved by what I see."

"I'm not moved by what I see," Estelle said in unison with the congregation.

"I'm not moved by what I feel!"

"I'm not moved by what I feel," Estelle once again spoke in unison with the congregation.

"Pray with me. God, we come to you this morning, first and foremost thanking you for waking us up this morning. Some did not wake up on this side of Heaven this morning and we ask that you be with the Whitfield family, as their nephew Zavion did not wake up this morning after suffering a stroke last night. We know that you are a comforter. We know that you can bring peace to their hearts in their time of grief. Let them not forget that you are always near. We ask a special prayer for the Jeffries family whose daughter was born two months early. We ask that you be a present guest in their daughter's room as you continually breathe life into her tiny body. We claim that she will grow stronger and stronger each day. Let her life be a testimony to your healing power that those who don't know you will know you through the miracle you are performing in her life. Lastly, God, but certainly not least, we lift up Sister Mae this morning, who will be having surgery this week. You are the great physician, the one who heals, and the one who restores. We know that you are making all things new in her body and she will come out of her surgery whole, nothing missing and nothing broken. In the mighty name of Jesus I pray, amen."

"Amen," the congregation said.

As the service went on, Estelle stood to walk to the women's restroom. Walking to the back of the church, she saw Farrah and Lewis sitting together. The two gave her a warm, welcoming smile, which she returned. Walking further back, she spotted Jada. Jada! Her friend and colleague had shown up to church. She was thankful to God for that. Estelle's gentle persistence in inviting Jada to church had worked. Estelle had been praying. When Estelle got all the way to the back before exiting the church to enter the vestibule where the restrooms were located, she was pleasantly surprised to see Kenneth sitting in the last pew with his sister Rhonda. Smiling, Estelle placed her hand on Kenneth's shoulder as she exited the church.

What a surprise, Estelle thought to herself as she washed her hands in the women's restroom. An unexpected surprise, but definitely a good one. She wondered when he had slipped in. She was too engrossed in praise and worship to notice if he had arrived then or later. She would ask him after service was over. Giving one final look at herself in the full-length mirror, Estelle found herself wondering how Kenneth knew that she attended church there. Per Farrah's advice, she had never mentioned it in conversation. She put two and two together, realizing that Kenneth wasn't there for her, but had been led there by God. He had mentioned that he was looking for a church home. Would God make this Kenneth's church home?

Returning to her seat, Estelle prepared her mind and heart to receive the message.

After service, Estelle made her way to where Jada was sitting.

Hugging her friend, Estelle said, "I'm so happy you're here."

"I'm so happy to be here," Jada said smiling. "So, this is what I've been missing all this time. The message was powerful."

"I'm glad you enjoyed the message."

"Yes, I did," Jada said, grabbing hold of Estelle's hand and hugging her friend again. "I can't thank you enough, Estelle, for speaking into my life. For showing me who God is and sharing with me how much Jesus loves me. Thank you, Estelle."

"Jada, Jada, Jada," Estelle said, stepping back to look at her friend. "Jesus looks good on you."

"Don't make me cry," Jada said.

"Hey, Jada! Hey, Estelle!" Farrah said hugging Jada and Estelle. "Jada, you are over here glowing! Nothing like being saved in Christ! Yeeees, girl!"

Smiling, Jada said, "Yes, I feel great."

"You look great, too," Farrah said. "You're wearing those pumps."

"Thanks," Jada said. "You look great, too."

"Thank you," Farrah said. "This outfit is straight off the rack from the outlet store."

"Farrah, you are too much," Estelle said.

As the three friends laughed, Kenneth and Rhonda joined them. With her back facing Kenneth, Jada and Farrah noticed him before Estelle did.

"Hello, Miss Blackwell," Kenneth spoke softly. "And hello to you two ladies. You must be Jada and Farrah. I've heard a lot about the both of you. Nice to meet you."

"Nice to meet you too, Dr. Alexander," Farrah said, extending her hand to shake his.

"Please, call me Kenneth. This is my sister Rhonda."

"Hello, Kenneth. Hello, Rhonda," Jada said smiling.

"Hello," Rhonda said to all three women.

"Hello, Kenneth and Rhonda," Estelle said, hugging the two. "It's so nice that you attended service today. May I ask how you heard of this church?"

"One of Rhonda's co-workers is a member here and she invited Rhonda. Then Rhonda invited me. And here I am here now with you."

Glancing at Farrah and then at Jada, smooth, Estelle thought to herself.

"It's so nice having you two here. Did you enjoy the service?" Farrah asked.

"Yes," Rhonda answered. "The spirit of the Lord filled the place. It was a great sermon. I truly appreciate a teaching pastor. Your pastor truly knows God's word." Switching her focus to Estelle, she said, "You have an anointed voice. Just beautiful."

Before Estelle could reply Kenneth spoke, "Yes, beautiful, just like you."

Blushing Estelle said, "Thank you."

"You're welcome," Kenneth said. "What do you ladies have planned? Rhonda and I were heading down to enjoy some Italian cuisine in the Lakefront. Would you three like to join us?"

Waiting for Estelle to answer first, Estelle said yes, followed by Jada answering yes.

"It's a yes for me, too," Farrah said. "I just need to find my husband."

"Sounds great," Kenneth said. "Rhonda and I will head out and meet you all at the restaurant. See you in a few."

"Yes, see you in a few, Kenneth," Estelle said as Kenneth and Rhonda walked out of the church.

"Go on with your bad self, Estelle, having an impromptu lunch with Dr. Kenneth Alexander," Jada said, giggling.

"Jada, you're a mess," Estelle said, laughing heartily. "But, a beautiful mess."

CHAPTER FIFTEEN

"We're having lunch with the doctor, with the doctor," Jada chanted as she and Estelle pulled into a parking space near the Italian restaurant. "We're having lunch with the doctor, with the doctor."

Giving Jada a serious side eye, Estelle said, "I really hope you'll be on your best behavior there."

"Now come on, Estelle, why wouldn't I be?"

"Because it's you."

"I'm insulted," Jada said.

"Please tell someone who would believe you," Estelle said, removing her key from the ignition.

Tapping the window of Estelle's car, Farrah motioned for her to open the door.

Opening the door for her, Farrah said, "Hurry up, Estelle. You can't keep the good doctor waiting."

Looking at Farrah, at Jada and then back at Farrah again, Estelle spoke, "The both of you are ridiculous."

"All I'm saying is to hurry and not keep the good doctor waiting," Farrah said, appalled by Estelle's comment.

Grinning while holding the door for the three friends to walk into the restaurant, Lewis said, "After you ladies."

Glancing around the restaurant, Estelle saw Kenneth waving to get their attention. Kenneth and Rhonda were seated at a large, rectangular table for eight. Estelle and her friends walked toward the table.

Pulling out a chair for Estelle next to him, Kenneth said, "Please, have a seat."

"Thank you, Kenneth," Estelle said.

"Jada, for you," Kenneth said, pulling out a chair for her as well.

"Thank you," Jada said.

"Kenneth, Rhonda, let me introduce you to Lewis, Farrah's husband," Estelle said as Lewis sat down after pulling a chair out for his wife.

"It's nice to meet the both of you," Lewis said. "Glad you could join us for service today. Would love to have you back."

"Yes, I can see that happening," Kenneth said, smiling at Estelle. "Shall we begin with some appetizers?"

"Most def," Lewis said, opening his menu. "Farrah and I love their calamari. Everyone good with that?"

"Calamari is my favorite," Rhonda said.

"Fine with me," added Jada.

"Me, too," Estelle said.

"Calamari it is and how about we throw in some chicken, spinach and bacon flatbread," Kenneth said.

"Sounds good to me," Lewis said as everyone nodded in agreement.

As everyone looked through their menu, a brunette waitress walked to their table.

"Good afternoon," she said. "Can I start you off with appetizers and beverages?"

"Yes," Kenneth answered. "We'll have the calamari and the chicken, spinach and bacon flatbread."

Writing, the waitress made eye contact with Estelle, "And what can I get you to drink?"

"I'll have a white peach palmer," Estelle answered.

"And for you," the waitress asked, directing her attention to Kenneth.

"I'll have a wild berry lemonade."

"And for you, miss?"

"I'll also have a wild berry lemonade," Rhonda said.

The waitress made eye contact with Jada who said, "I'll have a small mineral water."

"I'll have the same as her," Farrah said.

"And I'll have a lemonade," Lewis said.

"Thank you," the waitress said smiling. "I'll return with your appetizers and drinks shortly."

"How are you settling into Pittsburgh?" Lewis asked, directing his question to Kenneth.

"Well," Kenneth said. "I'm loving the city, the parks, my new home and new job. I'm settling in well. Thanks."

"Rhonda, how about you?" Jada asked. "How are you settling in? Kenneth said that your co-worker invited you to church. Where are you employed, if you don't mind me asking?"

"No, I don't mind you asking," Rhonda spoke kindly. "I am a CRNP in the maternity ward at the women's hospital in Oakland."

"Nice," Farrah chimed in. "That's where Sylvia from church works as an RN."

"Yes, that's who invited me."

"And as far as settling in," Farrah said. "What do you enjoy doing around the city?"

"I'm loving the restaurants and the arts. I love theatre."

"Me, too," Jada said.

"You know, Rhonda, Jada is a dance professor at the same university as Estelle," Kenneth said as the waitress returned to the table with their appetizers and drinks.

"You are?" Rhonda asked.

"Yes."

"Ballet?"

"Yes," Jada said.

"Very nice," Rhonda said.

"Thank you," Jada responded.

"We'll have to attend a play together some time."

"Yes, we should," Jada said.

"Make sure we exchange numbers before we go," Rhonda said.

"I will."

"Lewis, what do you do?" Kenneth asked.

"I'm a painter. I own my own business painting houses."

"Nice. I know who to call when I decide to have my house painted. Interior or exterior?"

"I do both," Lewis said. "Just let me know. I'll give you a good quote."

"Sounds good," Kenneth said.

As the group of old friends mixed with new friends enjoyed their conversation, the waitress returned to their table to take their order. The afternoon continued with laughter.

"Thanks for the invite," Lewis said to Kenneth. "We'll definitely need to get together again."

"Yes, we do," Kenneth said. "It was nice."

"Yes, it was," Farrah said to Rhonda. "It was so nice meeting the both of you."

"It was nice meeting you all also," Rhonda said.

"Rhonda, let me put your number in my phone," Jada said.

"Ready?" Rhonda asked.

"Yes."

Gently placing his hand beneath her elbow, Kenneth pulled Estelle to the side as his sister spoke with Jada and Farrah.

"When I woke up this morning and decided to accept my sister's invite to a new church, I didn't imagine that we would see one another today. But, let me say, I am very glad that we did. You look beautiful today, as always," Kenneth said, never losing eye contact with Estelle. "And your voice. Words can't describe. There's something about a woman who worships God."

"Yes, it was an unexpected, but pleasant surprise seeing you sitting in the pew in the church," Estelle said, still thinking how Kenneth was flirting with her. "You look very handsome yourself."

"Thank you, Dr. Blackwell."

"You're welcome, Dr. Alexander."

Smiling at Estelle and taking her hand into his, Kenneth said, "I don't want to keep you from your friends too much longer. Can I call you later?"

"Yes," Estelle said. "Yes, you can call me later."

"Until later," Kenneth said gently letting go of her hand. "Rhonda, are you ready?"

"Yes, brother," Rhonda said jokingly. "Bye, everyone."

"Bye," everyone said.

"Bye," Kenneth said to Farrah, Jada, Lewis and Estelle; never taking his eye off of Estelle.

"Yeees, Estelle, he's definitely a keeper," Farrah said as Estelle watched Kenneth walk away.

CHAPTER SIXTEEN

"What is so urgent that you needed me to rush over here immediately?" Estelle asked as she walked into Jada's apartment.

"Just come with me," Jada said, pulling Estelle by the arm down the hall into the bathroom, which was the last door on the left.

Confused, Estelle asked, "And can I ask why we are standing in your bathroom together?"

"Look," Jada said frantically.

Still not understanding, Estelle asked, "Jada, what am I looking at?"

Picking up a white stick from the sink counter, Jada repeated, "Look."

"You have a positive pregnancy test," Estelle said excitedly. "You're having a baby! Jada, you're having a baby!"

Taken aback by Estelle's response, Jada said, "Not exactly the response I expected from you. But, okay."

"What do you mean not the response you expected from me?"

Walking out of the bathroom with Estelle right behind her, Jada said angrily, "Yeah, like I said, not the response I expected from you. Not the response I expected from the woman who was pregnant and lost her baby. Not the response I expected from the woman whose husband had a baby with another woman. And definitely not the response I expected from the saved woman whose newly saved friend is having a baby out of wedlock. Don't people like you look down on people like me?"

"Jada, I know you don't mean any of that," Estelle spoke calmly. "This is just your fear speaking. You're afraid."

"You're wrong, Estelle," Jada said, fixing her gaze upon the floor. "I'm not afraid. I'm ashamed."

"Ashamed?" Estelle asked. "I have never known you to be ashamed."

Shaking her head then lying on her carpeted living room floor, Jada said, "Well that was before I knew any better and even knew I should be ashamed. But, now that I know how wrong I was, now I'm ashamed. I just started going to your church and now this. Guess God couldn't forgive me. I should have known it was too good to be true."

Taking a seat on the floor beside her friend, Estelle spoke, "No, it's not too good to be true. In fact, it's true it's too good. You see, God doesn't forgive us because we deserve to be forgiven. He forgives us because He loves us so much. While we were yet sinners Christ died for us."

Lifting her head from the floor, Jada asked, "If God loves me so much and has forgiven me, then why did He allow me to get pregnant?"

"Jada, when God forgives us, it doesn't mean that the consequences of our actions are taken away. Besides, it could be worse. But, know this, even God says, children are a gift from Him. God separates a child from the sin. Your baby is your gift." Estelle said, patting her friend's back.

Leaning on her arms, which were crossed under her chin on the floor, Jada spoke softly, "Estelle, I am afraid. I'm afraid more than I ever was any other time in my life."

"Everything will be okay."

"How are you so sure?"

"Because God said it."

The words resonated in Estelle's mind as she drove home from Jada's apartment.

"Because God said it," Estelle spoke out loud. "Because God said it."

Pulling into her driveway, she still kept hearing the words over and over in her mind. The more she tried to think of something else, the more the words ran through her mind. She wondered why she couldn't get those four words out of her mind. It was a bit concerning.

"God, if there's something you're trying to reveal to me, give me the spiritual eyes to see," Estelle spoke out loud again.

Closing the door behind her and locking it, she proceeded upstairs. She had had a long day and just wanted to relax. When she entered her bedroom, she didn't bother to switch the light switch on. There was always something about the quiet of the night that calmed her. Although she was a single woman who lived alone, she was never afraid. She trusted God and also had the added security of her years of mixed martial arts training along with her license to carry. But, above all, she trusted God to watch over her always.

After lying in her bed for a few minutes, she heard the notification that she had received a text message. The first ding was followed by another ding, then another, yet another.

Picking up her phone that laid on the bed beside her, Estelle said to herself, "Oh, Jada. She's probably worrying herself and can't sleep."

"Hey. Can't sleep. Thinking of you. I wonder if you think of me too. I miss you, Estelle. I miss you very much. I miss how much you loved me. I miss the home cooked meals. I miss your kisses, your touch. Do you miss those things too, Estelle? Maybe one day we could try again. Do you ever get lonely, Estelle? Like right now? Alone in our home in our bed alone. I'm lonely, Estelle. I want you. I can still hear your voice. I see you in my dreams. Do you still wear that long, flowy dress that I loved? Your booty and breasts always looked so good in it. I'm thinking of the way you look in it right now as I send this text. Can you ever forgive the past? Can we have a fresh start? I'll never stop loving you. I need someone. I need you. Can you call me? I'll be waiting."

Wrong about her assumption of the text being from Jada, Estelle had received a text from Clyde.

"The audacity," Estelle spoke out loud.

He'll be waiting a lifetime to hear from me. I'm not calling him, she thought to herself. Maybe she should change her number like Jada had suggested. Estelle had listened to God's instructions on seeing Clyde one last time. Maybe it was time to change her number so that he could never contact her again. Estelle thought more and more about what she should do and thought that maybe she should sell the house and move. If Clyde had no problem calling and texting her even after she said not to, what would stop him from showing up unexpectedly? Estelle didn't like the feeling that accompanied her thoughts. She did have the locks changed, but that wouldn't stop Clyde from showing up unannounced. Within the last few months, she had gone back and forth about moving, but never felt at peace about it until now. That's what she would do, she would move.

"You're going to move? To where?" Farrah asked.

"I haven't decided yet," Estelle said. "I just know I want to move. I need to. This was the home I shared with Clyde. I need a fresh start."

"I understand it all; get rid of all the emotional and material baggage."

"Yes, exactly. The only item that wasn't in this home when Clyde lived in it is my bed."

"You know I'm here when you decide you want to put your house on the market," Farrah said.

"Yes, I know. I will definitely let you know. You're the best realtor ever."

"And this is true," Farrah said smiling. "Clyde definitely needs prayer. His mind and heart are warped. Lord, help him. Do you pray for Clyde, Estelle?"

"Yes. I do. I didn't at first. I was too hurt. But, I do now."

"Good," Farrah said. "Even though you and Clyde are divorced, God doesn't want you to stop being concerned about his salvation. God allows us to break ties from toxic people, but our praying for them must never cease."

"Yes, Farrah, I know," Estelle said with a yawn.

"You know, Estelle, I am proud of you. Praying for our enemies is the toughest thing to do, yet you have drawn strength from God to do it."

CHAPTER SEVENTEEN

"Because God said it" kept going through Estelle's mind over the next few days, although she couldn't figure out why. She kept thinking about it as she prepared for her date with Kenneth.

"Have you ever kept having a recurring message play itself over and over in your mind, but you couldn't figure out the meaning behind the message?" Estelle asked.

Placing his fork on his plate and dabbing his mouth with his napkin, Kenneth answered, "Yes. Yes, I have."

"Ever since I left Jada's, the words *because God said it* keeps playing over and over in my mind. I keep praying for God to reveal the meaning to me, but I haven't received an answer yet."

"Then keep praying and waiting. He may reveal it to you now or He may reveal it to you later. But, in the interim I say to be still. Now isn't the time to make any big decisions. Be still."

"Yes, I need to be still," Estelle agreed.

"How is your omelet?"

"It's so good," Estelle said after chewing. "The bacon mixed with the avocado and Monterey Jack cheese taste so good. It's delicious. I'm glad you brought me here for breakfast. Thank you. How is your meal?"

"I'm satisfied, completely satisfied. It's like art for the palette. The Italian sausage mixed with the red peppers, roasted tomatoes and red peppers and herbs is so tasty. The mozzarella and parmesan cheeses make it even better."

"What are your plans for the rest of the day?" Estelle asked, observing other patrons of the café-style restaurant being seated.

"A few colleagues of mine and I are going to play a little three-on-three at the gym this afternoon. Get some cardio in. After the overly stressful week I had in surgery I need some physical exercise to get rid of some of this stress."

"Surgery was overly stressful this past week?" Estelle asked.

"Yes," Kenneth said. "Let's just say that everything that could go wrong went wrong during several surgeries this week. But, I'm thankful to God that He guides my hands; that He guides my mind. No matter what complications arise during any of the surgeries I perform, God keeps me in perfect peace. There is no room for panic in the operating room."

"Yes, it's only God who can speak to us in stressful moments to help us get through. You just happen to be in a profession where the stress is higher than most other professions."

"I'm sure you can relate to the stress that comes along with a profession," Kenneth said. "It has to be difficult teaching a large number of individuals, who all learn differently. You have to teach in such a way that everyone will understand."

"Yes, I struggled with that a lot in my beginning years as a professor. I still come across it at times now," Estelle said. "Like when every student does poorly on an exam or a high percentage of the students don't understand a theory. As a professor, you have to be willing to admit that somewhere in translation, your teaching simply was not clear. I know many professors who never admit that about themselves."

"Speaking of clear, Professor Blackwell, I would like to discuss our relationship," Kenneth said, looking intently into Estelle's eyes.

Estelle knew this discussion would eventually arise, but she didn't expect it today. She was caught totally off guard.

"Yes, Kenneth, what would you like to discuss?" Estelle asked.

"Our exclusivity. When I court a woman, I like to be exclusive. I've never been a man to date multiple women at once, even before I gave my life to Christ. It was never my desire."

"I understand. I'm the same way when dating men."

"The two of us have been enjoying each other's company these last few months and I just want to be clear on the direction the two of us want this to go," Kenneth said, taking a sip of his orange juice. "Estelle, you're a beautiful, intelligent, Jesus-loving woman. That's what I like about you. As a man I believe it is important for me to be clear about my intentions with a woman."

"Kenneth, I enjoy spending time with you, too. These last couple of months have been great. You're handsome, Kenneth, very handsome. Your love of Christ and your desire to serve God is refreshing. And you're definitely smart. Very smart," Estelle said.

Reaching across the table and taking Estelle's hand into his, Kenneth said, "Estelle, we're friends now, enjoying time together, getting to know one another. I can easily see this turning into more. I can see a courtship in our future. Do you see the same, Estelle?"

"I could see that," Estelle said, placing her other hand on top of his.

"As we continue getting to know one another more and more, I could see marriage in our future," Kenneth said. "Now I don't want you to get nervous, Estelle. This by no means is a marriage proposal. I wouldn't rush you into that. I just wanted to let you know how I feel and my intentions."

"I'm not nervous. I know what you mean."

"Good. You can respond now if you like, but if you need some time to respond to this, I respect that."

"Thank you. I really do like you, Kenneth, but, yes, I do need some time."

CHAPTER EIGHTEEN

"He asked you to marry him?" Jada asked.

"No, Kenneth said that he could see marriage in our future," Estelle said, removing her sandals and lying on Jada's couch. It was Sunday afternoon and Estelle and Jada decided to relax at Jada's apartment after church for the afternoon.

"And what did you say?"

"I didn't say anything," Estelle said shyly.

"You didn't say anything? A man who is handsome, intelligent and paid, and above all loves Christ, tells you that he sees marriage to you in his future and you say nothing?" Jada asked skeptically. "Girl, if I didn't know you earned a PhD, I would think you were all kind of stupid."

Laughing, Estelle said, "All kind of stupid? That's how we're approaching this? Jada, I can't deal with you."

"But, you will," Jada said smiling. "But, for real, why didn't you say anything?"

"You know, Jada, I really don't know."

"Well, even if you don't know the reason, you didn't say anything. What's done is done," Jada said. "Let's eat. I have a taste for loaded nachos."

Following Jada into her small kitchen, Estelle thought about Clyde's text message. "Clyde contacted me again," Estelle said as she took a seat at Jada's small kitchen table.

"Why doesn't that dude get a clue?"

"Your guess is as good as mine. I need to read the text to you verbatim," Estelle said, retrieving her cell out of the pocket of her dress.

"Yes, please," Jada said, removing food storage containers filled with leftover ingredients for loaded nachos from the refrigerator. "Not a single word needs to be left out."

"The text reads, 'Hey. Can't sleep. Thinking of you. I wonder if you think of me too. I miss you, Estelle. I miss you very much. I miss how much you loved me. I miss the home cooked meals. I miss your kisses, your touch. Do you miss those things too, Estelle?" Estelle said. "Then he even has the nerve to say, maybe one day we could try again. Do you ever get lonely, Estelle? Like right now? Alone in our home in our bed alone. I'm lonely, Estelle. I want you. I can still hear your voice. I see you in my dreams. Do you still wear that long, flowy dress that I loved? He then had the audacity to say, your booty and breast always looked so good in it. I'm thinking of the way you look in it right now as I send this text. Can you ever forgive the past? Can we have a fresh start? I'll never stop loving you. I need someone. I need you. Can you call me? I'll be waiting."

Placing the container of ground meat on the counter that she was about to place in the microwave, Jada looked at Estelle and said, "He said he'll be waiting? Who does this dude think he is? Some lost treasure? I don't know how you put up with him?"

"Only by God's grace."

Opening the microwave and placing the container inside, Jada said, "Well, I'm new to this God's grace stuff. If I was in your situation and I told a guy not to contact me and he kept contacting me, I would accept his invitation to meet up with him and when he would show up, a few of my male cousins would be waiting to dust him off."

"Dust him off," Estelle said, chuckling.

"I don't know why you're sitting there laughing, Estelle," Jada said, removing the container when the microwave timer beeped. "I'm so serious. Danny, Andy and Walter would dust him off. I bet a dude would think twice before he dialed my number again."

"Think twice," Estelle said, shaking her head. "A man with any sense would delete your number from their contacts."

"Well, you know, Estelle, that there are some who don't have the sense God gave them. And there are some who still wouldn't have sense if it was placed on a shelf with a price tag of free. That ex of yours is one of them. He doesn't have any sense."

"I don't disagree with you about that," Estelle said as Jada placed a heaping plate of nachos in front of her.

"I know you said you're dealing with this by God's grace. What does that mean?"

"Grace when it concerns salvation means that God extended underserved love to us. But grace as it pertains to how I'm dealing with this situation is God's grace gives me guidance. His grace gives me strength. His grace keeps my sanity through all of this."

Placing the ground meat on top of the nachos along with the other toppings, Jada took a seat at the table and said, "God's grace would need to keep me from punching Clyde in the face. Let's eat."

When Estelle arrived home, she began walking through the rooms of her home sorting her belongings. She had a pile to be donated and a pile to be thrown away. Each room in her home had a pile in it. She didn't have a keep pile in each room because she knew exactly what she would keep, her clothes, shoes, accessories and her grandmother's teapot. None of the material items in her home that she once shared with Clyde mattered to her. She was fine letting them go. The process was freeing. In her living room was a pile of wall décor, lamps and a rolled-up throw rug to donate. Hers and Clyde's wedding album lay in a pile alone to be thrown away. In her kitchen was a pile of dishes and silverware to be donated. In Estelle's upstairs hallway out of her linen closet were washcloths, towels, pillowcases and bed sheets to be tossed. After Estelle sorted items in each room of the house, she retreated to her bedroom and called Farrah.

"Farrah, are you busy tomorrow?" Estelle asked.

"No," Farrah answered.

"What about Lewis? Is he busy tomorrow?"

"No, Estelle. Is everything okay?" Farrah asked.

"Yes, everything is fine. Can you and Lewis come to my house tomorrow morning around 10?"

"Yes," Farrah said. "Are you sure everything is okay?"

"Yes, I'm sure, Farrah. I'll see you two tomorrow. I'll explain everything then," Estelle said, ending their call.

CHAPTER NINETEEN

"Estelle, may I ask, what is all of this?" Farrah asked as she made her way around piles of her friend's belongings.

"What does it look like?"

"It looks like all of your stuff in piles," Farrah said confused. "But, why?"

"Yeah, why?" Lewis asked, just as confused.

"It is all of my stuff in piles," Estelle said smiling. "There are two piles in each room and hallway. One pile is to be thrown away. The other pile is to be donated."

"Okay," Lewis said, taking a seat on the couch while looking at the piles in front of him. "But that still isn't telling us why."

"Are you having a nervous breakdown, Estelle?" Farrah asked. "Lewis, we may need to get her down to Eastern Psych."

"Farrah, I am absolutely fine. In fact, I haven't felt this good in a long time," Estelle said.

"Are you sure you feel fine? Are you sick? Maybe you're febrile," Farrah said placing her hand on Estelle's forehead.

"Farrah, I'm okay," Estelle said, still smiling.

"If you're not sick. If you're not having a mental breakdown, then what is wrong with you?" Lewis asked. "What's your explanation for all of this, Estelle?"

"Philippians three."

"Philippians three?" Farrah asked, taking a seat next to her husband, still confused.

"That doesn't explain anything," Lewis said. "That's a whole chapter in the Bible. You're gonna need to give us a little more than that."

"Philippians three verses thirteen and fourteen."

Taking a moment to think, Lewis said, "I press!"

Giving Lewis a side eye, Farrah said, "Lewis, I press?"

"Yes," Lewis said. "Estelle is referring to the *I press* scripture in Philippians."

"Are you?" Farrah asked Estelle skeptically.

"Yes, I am," Estelle said. "Lewis is right. I am forgetting about what has passed and looking ahead of what is to come. I press toward the goal. I'm paraphrasing of course."

"And what may I ask does that scripture have to do with this mess you have made all over your house?" Farrah asked.

"Let me answer your question for her," Lewis said standing, walking over to Estelle and draping his arm over her shoulder. "May I?"

"If you must," Estelle said, taking a seat next to her friend. The two looked up to Lewis as he began to speak.

"You said you're forgetting about what has passed and looking ahead of what is to come; you press toward the goal. Farrah, what Estelle is saying is that she is forgetting about Clyde, her past. She's looking ahead at what is to come, which is all of God's blessings and promises. She's pressing toward that goal."

Jumping up from the couch and high fiving Lewis, Estelle shouted joyfully, "You got it!"

"I'm glad he got it," Farrah said, shaking her head.

"That's right. I got it, babe," Lewis said, kissing Farrah on her forehead.

"So, let's get to work," Estelle said, handing a garbage bag and box to each of them. "The donate piles go in the boxes. The throw-away piles go in the garbage bags."

Starting to pick up items off of the floor, Farrah looked around, still confused, "That's basically everything."

"Exactly," Estelle said, heading up the stairs.

"I truly appreciate the two of you helping me," Estelle said as the three friends sat in her living room seeing what they had accomplished.

"I'm glad we could help," Farrah said. "I didn't understand it at first, but now I do. It's freeing."

"Yes, it is," Estelle said.

"Freeing and tiring," Lewis added with a chuckle. "I believe I got my workout in for the week."

Farrah smiled at her husband lovingly, then said, "Yes, she did put us to work."

"Since my work here is done, I'm going to leave you ladies to yourselves. I'm going to head home for a nap. A brother is tired."

"Thanks again, Lewis," Estelle said.

"I'll see you later. Love you," Farrah said as Lewis walked out the door.

"I'm going to change my cell number," Estelle said. "Jada had asked me a while back why I didn't change my number when Clyde contacted me early on. At the time I was following what God was telling me to do. And now I am going to change my number *because God said it*. Oh, my goodness, Farrah!"

"Estelle, what is it?"

"For a while now I've been trying to figure out why the words *because God said it* kept playing over and over in my mind. All along, the way I have been dealing with Clyde is *because God said it*. I didn't change my number and asked him to meet me at the coffee shop to tell him not to contact me again…"

"*Because God said it*," Farrah said catching on.

"Yes. And I got rid of all of my belongings…"

"*Because God said it*," the two friends said in unison.

"None of this is about Clyde. All of this has been about me and God. It's about me walking daily with Him and knowing that He knows best and that I can trust Him."

"I am so happy for you, Estelle," Farrah said hugging her friend. "I really am."

"And now I also know how to answer Kenneth, *because God said it*," Estelle said.

CHAPTER TWENTY

Riding her bike along the river trail on a warm August day, Estelle thought about how summer was coming to an end and the fall semester would be starting soon. The last few years between today and her separation had been an emotional roller coaster. Receiving the divorce papers earlier in the year had been eye opening. The last few months had been her growth period. She was looking forward to growing more each day. Estelle was learning to live her life with expectancy, knowing that when she walked hand-in-hand with God, her life would reflect His goodness. She looked forward to more personal growth and growing closer to Christ. Her thoughts brought her to Kenneth. For this reason, Estelle knew what her response would be to what Kenneth said over dinner. Estelle would express the stage of life that she was in when she met up with Kenneth later that evening.

Returning her bike to the young man working at the bike rental shop, Estelle made her way to her car for her drive home. A warm shower awaited her. Thinking about a nice lunch of cold pasta salad, baked chicken and a tall glass of lemonade made her stomach growl.

When Estelle arrived home, there was a medium-sized package sitting on her porch. She couldn't recall recently placing an online order and wondered what it could be and who it could be from. Stepping onto the landing of the porch, she noticed the box was from one of her favorite Pittsburgh clothing boutiques. Picking up the box and taking it inside, she couldn't wait to see what awaited her.

Sitting on the couch, which would be gone later that afternoon along with her other furniture, Estelle placed the box on the floor and opened it. She removed a tropical print caftan. It was absolutely beautiful. Reaching further into the box, she removed a personalized note from an envelope. It read:

Estelle,

My friend, my sister... a little back to "school" gift for a regal gal like you. Thank you for introducing me to Jesus. He is the best thing that has ever happened to me.

Jada

Reaching for her cell phone, which was lying on the couch next to her, Estelle dialed Jada's number.

"Hey, Estelle," Jada said.

"Hey, Jada," Estelle said, laying the caftan across the couch to get a better look at it. "Thank you for the gift. It's beautiful."

"You're welcome. Recently I was in the vicinity of your favorite boutique and I decided to look around. You know, see if there was anything that I liked. I bought a nice designer bag for myself," Jada said. "Then I saw the caftan and just knew you would like it. I'm glad you like it."

"I don't just like it. I really like it. I'm definitely wearing it on the first day of classes."

"I'm glad."

"Again, thank you so much."

"You're welcome," Jada said happily. "What's your plans for today?"

"The movers should be here shortly to take all of my furniture. I'm donating it all to the mission store. Then I'm meeting Kenneth. You?"

"I'm relaxing today. This morning sickness is on some gangsta stuff. It's brutal," Jada said, chuckling. "But, for real, I don't know how women go through multiple pregnancies. It's one and done for me."

"One and done?" Estelle asked, laughing.

"Yes, one and done," Jada repeated, laughing too. "I'll talk with you later. I know you have the movers coming soon. Have a good time with Kenneth. Again, I'm glad you like your gift. Bye."

"Bye," Estelle said, ending the call.

As Estelle watched the movers drive away with her belongings, she felt a surge of peace sweep over her.

"Wow," Estelle spoke out loud, closing the door behind her.

After finishing her shower, standing with her plush bathrobe on in front of her bedroom closet choosing what to wear, Estelle liked this feeling of peace. She hadn't felt completely at peace in a long time. Getting dressed, she chose a pair of skinny jeans to wear with a graphic tee. Wrapping her hair in a head wrap, she tied her outfit all together with a pair of lace-less, canvas sneakers. Giving herself a final head-to-toe look-over in her full-length mirror, she was ready to go.

Unlocking her car, Estelle placed an overnight bag in the trunk. Hopping into the driver's seat and starting the ignition of her car, she pulled out of the driveway. Estelle felt confident and at peace with the decision she was going to make today.

Pulling into the parking lot, Estelle looked around at all of the cars. It took her ten minutes to find a parking space. The place was packed. Unbuckling her seatbelt, she stepped out of her car, activated the locks and proceeded to meet Kenneth at the top of the escalators.

As the escalator ascended, Kenneth came into view. He stood at the top dressed in a pair of knee-length shorts, a red polo shirt, white sneakers and a fitted cap. The good doctor looked nice, Estelle thought to herself.

"I'm loving your graphic tee," Kenneth said. "A nice throwback to our youth."

"Thank you," Estelle said. "I used to love the show as a kid."

"How are you?"

"I'm good," Estelle said. "All of my furniture was hauled away earlier; every last piece."

"How did that make you feel?"

Turning to look directly at Kenneth, Estelle said, "It made me feel free."

"Free," Kenneth said. "Such a good feeling."

"Yes," Estelle said, looking up at the sky and then back at Kenneth. "It's a beautiful day."

"Yes, it is," Kenneth said. "Shall we walk?"

"Yes, let's go see the animals," Estelle said, smiling.

Walking slowly along the uphill, winding path of the zoo, Estelle thought about what she was going to discuss with Kenneth today. Should she say it now or should she wait? She decided to wait.

"Where would you like to go next? To the aquarium or to see the reptiles?"

"Easy answer, the aquarium. Reptiles make me cringe," Estelle said; scrunching her shoulders to her neck. "I never liked them."

Smiling, Kenneth said, "To the aquarium we go, Miss Reptiles Make Me Cringe."

Shrugging her shoulders and smiling, Estelle said, "That's me."

"I love the tropical fish. Seeing them always reminds me of when I went snorkeling in the Bahamas. It was hands down, one of the best experiences of my life. Everything was just so beautiful," Estelle said as she and

Kenneth walked, gazing at the many fish within the indoor aquarium.

"I agree. Snorkeling is amazing," Kenneth said as the two neared a bench sitting directly in front of one of the fish displays. "Shall we sit?"

"Sure," Estelle said, taking a seat beside Kenneth. "Where did you go snorkeling?"

"Hawaii, Key West, La Jolla Cove off the coast of San Diego, Seychelles Islands off the coast of Kenya and Norman Reef, Australia," Kenneth said with a smile.

"I'm impressed, Dr. Alexander. Kenya and Norman Reef. Major points for you," Estelle said. "Impressive."

"Thank you," Kenneth said enjoying that he could impress Estelle. "Being able to go snorkeling is one of the top activities that need to be available when I visit a place. I enjoyed snorkeling in Hawaii, Key West and La Jolla Cove during some free time while attending work conferences. I got lucky. Just like when I met you."

"Lucky?" Estelle said, laughing. "I wouldn't call it lucky. Especially not on my end. You treated my sprained ankle the first time we met. Remember? If not, I sure do."

"I definitely remember. And my back does, too," Kenneth said, laughing.

"I am all muscle weight," Estelle said looking at him from the side and elbowing him jokingly. "You know it's true."

"If you say so," Kenneth said, smiling at Estelle.

Deciding that there was no better time than the moment they had sitting in the aquarium together, Estelle turned to Kenneth and said, "There's something I need to say to you."

"Yes, Estelle. What is it that you need to say?"

Estelle had rehearsed the words over and over in her mind, but that was it, she never said the words out loud and wasn't sure what the words would sound like audibly. But she was going to find out now.

"Kenneth, you know that I have enjoyed the time we have been spending together."

"Yes, as I have too."

"I really enjoy it," Estelle said, placing her hand upon his. "You're a good man, Kenneth. You love God. You're honest. You're kind. You're strong. You have the qualities any woman would want in a man."

Looking down at the floor and then staring at the aquarium, Kenneth said, "I have the qualities any woman would want in a man, but. I know there's a *but* coming in what you have to say."

"Yes, there is," Estelle spoke slowly. "You have the qualities any woman would want in a man but, I am not looking to be in a serious relationship and I know that's what you want. It's not the desire of my heart to cultivate a relationship for marriage. It's not where I'm at, at this point in my life."

Taking a moment to absorb all that she had said, Kenneth turned to look at her. "I respect that. I respect you. Although I wish I would have met you before Clyde, that's not what God intended. And now as we sit here together, as beautiful of a couple we would make, today our journey ends."

"Yes, Kenneth, it does," Estelle said, gently squeezing his hand. "You and I are simply on two different paths."

Softly kissing Estelle's hand, Kenneth said, "Yes, two different paths that were given the chance to converge, if only for a little while. I'm thankful for that."

CHAPTER TWENTY-ONE

"Are you okay?" Jada asked Estelle as she walked into the kitchen where Estelle was sitting drinking a cup of tea.

Looking up to see her friend, Estelle said, "Yes."

Taking a seat beside Estelle, Jada said, "I know it had to be hard for you to let Kenneth go."

"Yes," Estelle said. "Yes, it was. He's a good man. God knows he is. However, simply being a good man doesn't mean he's meant to be in my life."

"He saw the possibility of marriage to you in his future."

"That's exactly why I had to let Kenneth go," Estelle said, looking at Jada and then staring down into her cup of tea. "I've never been one to lead a man on. I sure wasn't going to start now. As much as I enjoyed spending time with Kenneth, when he started talking courtship and marriage, I knew what I had to do."

"But?" Jada asked. "For some reason I feel like that's what you're going to say next."

Smiling at Jada, Estelle said, "I was thinking it, but I've learned to stop wondering why or what if. Kenneth is such a good man; a Christian man. He's so unlike Clyde. But I made my decision, the decision I strongly believe God wanted me to make for this time in my life."

"Do you think you would ever consider getting married again at another time of your life?"

"You know, I could see a strong possibility that I could revisit the possibility of marriage again one day."

"Good, because I need to be in a wedding. I've never been in one," Jada said.

Laughing at her friend, Estelle said, "We'll visit that if we ever cross that bridge. But, for now, this time around in my life, I'm committing to a time of personal growth. Growing spiritually, mentally and emotionally is a process. I want to be sure that I get everything that God wants for me out of the process. At this point of the process in my life, it doesn't include a man. And you know what, Jada, I'm okay with that."

Smiling, Jada said, "If you're okay, then I'm okay. "I'll be right back. I need to go throw up."

Estelle was okay. For once in her life, she didn't need to try to convince herself that she was okay. She didn't have to pretend she was okay. She was genuinely okay. And she knew that Kenneth was okay, too. She prayed that he would continue to be successful as a surgeon. She also prayed that he would find love and marriage. Those were the desires of his heart and he truly deserved it.

"I hate morning sickness," Jada said, returning to the kitchen. "But, I'm glad you and I get to be roommates!"

"I am too. I appreciate you opening your home to me."

I know you are," Jada said. "Besides, I sure wasn't going to let you stay in a hotel while Farrah puts your house up for sale."

"I know."

I hope everything was okay for you sleeping in the guest room last night."

"It was," Estelle said. "The bed is so comfortable."

"Good," Jada said. "Did you already eat breakfast when I was still asleep?"

"Yes, I had toast with my tea. I just wanted something light. Would you like some toast? A banana? Something light for your stomach?" Estelle asked.

"I'll have some toast. No banana. Thanks," Jada said, getting up from the table. "I'm going to go relax in the recliner while I wait."

"Okay, I'll bring it in when it's ready," Estelle said as Jada walked sluggishly out of the kitchen.

"Just one slice, Estelle," Jada shouted from the living room. "I don't think my stomach can hold much more."

"Are you sure you don't want to eat two slices?"

"No," Jada said sleepily. "I can only handle one piece. I hope."

Walking into the living room with a slice of toast and a glass half filled with ginger ale on a tray, Estelle asked, "Is there anything else I can get for you?"

"Yes," Jada said. "Can you bring the ottoman over to the couch so I can prop my feet up?"

Picking up the small, circular ottoman, Estelle carried it to the couch where Jada was lying. "Here you go," Estelle said, taking a seat on the couch.

"Thank you," Jada said, moving from the recliner to the couch. "I can't get comfortable sitting in the recliner."

"Would you like some pillows behind your back?"

"No, thank you," Jada said.

"What do you say to us ordering in tonight? We both could use a break from cooking."

"Sounds good to me," Jada said, taking small bites of her lightly buttered toast and sips of her ginger ale.

"Are you sure you're okay?" Estelle asked. "You don't look well."

"Because I'm not, Estelle. This morning sickness is kicking my butt."

"I understand," Estelle said. "But, trust me, it gets better."

"Oh, I'm so sorry. All this time I'm complaining about morning sickness and not feeling well. It's so insensitive of me. I'm so sorry."

"Don't be. I've made peace with having a miscarriage. Don't ever apologize for your blessing. I'm just happy to be a part of this journey with you."

"I don't know how you do it, Estelle. Your strength is amazing," Jada said.

"Don't be amazed by me. God is the One who is amazing. It's His strength that lives in me," Estelle said. "And you know what, Jada, once you accepted Jesus into your heart, now God's strength lives in you."

CHAPTER TWENTY-TWO

I'm loving the changes you've made to your office," Estelle said, taking a seat on the opposite side of Farrah's desk. "It really looks beautiful in here."

"Thanks," Farrah said, removing a mug from the coffee maker and setting it in front of Estelle. "I had to make a decision between the boho chic look and minimalist look. You see which one won."

"Well, of course," Estelle said, laughing. "Nothing about you screams boho chic."

Laughing, Farrah said, "I know. That's why my former designer was fired."

"I never understood why you were paying a designer anyway. You stage houses all of the time and do well doing it. You could have put together your office yourself."

"You're exactly right," Farrah said. "And I love the look."

Taking a sip of her coffee, Estelle asked, "French toast?"

"Yes."

"Delicious," Estelle said, taking another sip.

Smiling, Farrah said, "I knew you would like it."

"Because you know me," Estelle said, setting her coffee mug on Farrah's desk. "That is the exact reason why you are the first to know that this will be my last semester teaching. After the fall semester I am opening my own counseling center."

"Estelle," Farrah said, a smile overtaking her face. I know you spoke of this years ago. I'm so happy for you."

"Yes, I'm happy too," Estelle said. "But I must admit, I'm nervous too. I will need all the advice I can get from you about running my own business. The counseling part comes first-hand to me. But the business side is foreign to me. I will need a lot of help."

"I'll help you in any way I can," Farrah said. "I am so excited. I know God is leading you down this road and He is going to bless your business."

"Thank you," Estelle said. "I'll need your help locating office space."

"I can absolutely do that," Farrah said, opening a manila folder. "Now about selling your house. I have shown it to many prospective buyers this past week. Many good offers have been coming in. It's down to two possible buyers. I'm confident I'll have your house sold soon. When I say soon, I mean in a matter of days."

"I am confident, too," Estelle said. "You're the best realtor in Pittsburgh."

"And you know this," Farrah said as the two friends laughed.

Walking along the busy street, Estelle thought about all that had transpired in the last year. She reflected upon the good and the bad. God had truly bought her through that which she felt would destroy her.

Stopping in front of a boutique to look at a turquoise dress on the mannequin in the window, Estelle felt overwhelmed with gratefulness to God.

"Thank you, God," Estelle spoke out loud, unconcerned with people passing by.

"Estelle," a woman's voice called.

Not knowing who the voice belonged to, Estelle turned around to see Clyde's girlfriend standing with her and Clyde's baby in a stroller beside her.

"Yes," Estelle replied, waiting for what she had to say.

"I thought that was you," she said.

"Yes, it's me," Estelle said, not knowing what else to say.

"How have you been?" she asked awkwardly.

"Good," Estelle answered, feeling uncomfortable. "And you?"

"Okay," she said. "No, I lied. I'm not okay. Clyde left us."

Still not knowing what to say, Estelle responded the best way she knew how by saying, "I'm sorry to hear that."

"He moved to Chicago. You know his mom lives out there now."

"No, I didn't know," Estelle said, looking around.

"Yeah, she moved back to her old childhood home in Chicago. Clyde lives there now. I never hear from him," she said.

"I really don't know what to say," Estelle admitted truthfully.

"I thought he loved me," she said.

"So did I," Estelle said. "But, like I said, I really don't know what you want me to say to all of this."

Taking a moment before speaking, she said, "Look, I saw you as I was walking down the street. The same feeling of intimidation came over me that I had always felt. I'm intimidated by you. You're smart. You're successful. You're beautiful. You're kind. You're everything I'm not."

"I'm sure there are good things about you," Estelle said with the same feeling of discomfort she had felt when the conversation began.

"Please, let me finish," she said. "When I saw how happy Clyde was with you and how great you were for him, you would think I would have stopped messing around with him."

"You think?" Estelle asked.

"Please, there's more," she said. "But, I didn't. You being so great just made me want Clyde more. He tried to break it off several times, but I wouldn't let him go."

"Thanks for sharing, but I have to go," Estelle said, attempting to walk away.

"Wait, please. There's more."

Reluctantly, Estelle said, "Go on."

"I wouldn't let him go. I couldn't," she said looking down at her feet and then back at Estelle. "I'm sorry."

Caught off guard by her unexpected words, Estelle took a deep breath and said, "Thank you. I forgive you."

"You forgive me?" she asked, confused.

"Yes," Estelle said. "I forgave you long before today. But, thank you for your apology."

"You did?"

"Yes," Estelle said. "God told me to forgive you. Lord knows I didn't want to. But, I did it because that's what God calls me to do. So, don't think about it anymore, I don't."

Placing her hands on the stroller, still in disbelief, she asked, "Is it that easy?"

"It's not easy," Estelle said. "But it is possible."

CHAPTER TWENTY-THREE

"Didn't I tell you that your house would be sold in a few days?" Farrah asked excitedly. "Did your girl deliver?"

"You sure did," Estelle said, loving the excitement in Farrah's voice. "I had no doubt about it."

"I know you are happy. And I'm so happy for you. God is truly giving you beauty for ashes."

"Yes," Estelle said. "God has given me joy for mourning."

"He has given you a garment of praise…"

"For the spirit of heaviness," Estelle said, finishing her friend's sentence. "God has been good to me."

"Yes," Farrah said. "Yes, He has."

"I'm so grateful," Estelle said.

"I know you are."

"I know you have to get back to working," Estelle said. "Thanks again."

"You're welcome," Farrah said.

Ending the call with Farrah, Estelle sat for a moment looking around her office before she clicked open an urgent interoffice email.

Estelle wondered what could be so urgent with the semester not even beginning yet.

Estelle read the email and then had to read it a second and third time. Her heart couldn't believe the news of what her eyes read in the email.

Dear Colleagues,

The Psychology Department is saddened to inform all staff and faculty of the psychology department of the passing of psychology major, Precious Lane. Precious Lane, 20, was called home on August 7. Lane passed away from natural causes. She was found unconscious by her family with her cause of death being a brain aneurysm. We, the faculty and staff, who had come to know Lane will remember her fondly.

Sincerely,

Charles Andrew, Psychology Department Chair

"Precious Lane," Estelle spoke her name softly.

"I couldn't stay in my office a minute longer without feeling like I would suffocate," Estelle said, lying back on the black chaise in Jada's office. "With tomorrow being the first day of classes, I can't stay on this campus much longer today."

"Precious Lane," Jada said. "Twenty years old. So hard to believe."

"She was brilliant," Estelle said. "Absolutely brilliant."

Sitting in silence for a moment thinking, Jada said, "Death, it's one thing I will never understand. She was only twenty years old."

"I just can't believe it," Estelle said, staring at the wall. "I can't believe it."

Tapping her friend on the shoulder, Jada said, "Come on, Estelle, let's get out of here."

Standing, Estelle asked, "Where are we going? Home?"

"No," Jada said. "I have someplace to show you."

"Let's go. I'm sure ready to get out of here. The weight of the bad news is in this place."

City streets turning to small town roads to highways then winding country roads, Estelle found herself in a place she had never been.

"Wow," Estelle said. "I've lived in Pennsylvania my entire life and have never heard of this place."

"You're among many who I tell about here that have never heard of it before," Jada said as the two friends stepped out of Jada's car, which she had parked in a grassy field. "Whitsett holds a special place in my heart. Let's walk."

Following her friend, Estelle felt calm; she felt at peace. Even with the sad news of the passing of her former student, away from the noise of the city, she felt peace.

"Watch your step," Jada said as she descended down a pair of wooden stairs that jutted out of the dirt.

As the two friends made their way down the stairs, once at the bottom, they found themselves in an open, sand-like clearing surrounded with trees.

"Welcome to the beach," Jada said smiling and twirling around.

It did, in fact, resemble a beach, Estelle thought to herself.

"And over there to your right would be the man with the big afro playing the guitar and singing reggae late into the night. And to your left you would find me sitting with my mother, childhood friends and their mother shucking corn," Jada said closing her eyes, freely dancing in the clearing. "The large pig roasting for all to see, the tree swing catapulting you into the river, the dirt between my toes, the breeze through my hair."

"Did you grow up here?" Estelle asked.

"My dad grew up here. I spent my summers here. Come on, follow me."

Following Jada down a sand-like slope that their feet sunk into, the two friends stood with a river in front of them.

Waving her arm out toward the river, as if to introduce the two, Jada said, "The Youghiogheny River. Or known to many as, the mighty, mighty Yough."

"Beautiful," Estelle said, taking it all in.

Walking along the riverbank, Jada spoke, "You never cross the same river twice. Just like the river, life is always changing. The river is powerful, it's cleansing, it's calm, it's raging, it's relentless, it's giving. But, overall, it's beautiful. All those things are life, too, and life is beautiful."

"Yes, it is," Estelle said.

"We don't know why Precious Lane had to die young," Jada said, holding a couple of smooth rocks in her hands. "But, two things we are sure of is that life is always changing, but God, He always stays the same. You taught me that, Estelle."

Tears falling from her eyes, Estelle bent her knees to slowly sit on the ground.

"He never changes," Estelle said through tear filled eyes.

"What you focus on consumes you," Jada said, kneeling beside Estelle. "Let God consume you."

"God, consume me," Estelle cried out; her hands raised high.

"Estelle, you are not moved by what you feel. And you won't start now. Yes, you're sad, but let that be the fuel to your fire. Don't be consumed by your feelings. Be consumed by the word of God. God's word says, His grace is sufficient. He's more than enough. God's more than enough."

CHAPTER TWENTY-FOUR

Fall semester had arrived. Estelle's last fall semester. Her very last semester ever, to be exact. Estelle was okay with that fact. She would give her last semester her very best, as she always did. Estelle was excited about what the incoming freshman class had to offer, in reference to smarts, not just book smarts, but everyday application type of smart, too.

"Good morning, class. Welcome to Psychology 101. Here you're not just another number. Here, you're a face. You're a name. You're a person. You're a beautiful mind. Teaching to me isn't simply a paycheck. Teaching, to me, has always been teaching the next set of brilliant minds," Estelle said leaning against a desk and then walking to her podium. "Here's to a great semester."

"How did your first class go?" Estelle asked Jada who sat in her chaise of her office with her feet propped up.

"Can you say doozy?" Jada said, giving Estelle the side eye.

"A doozy?" Estelle asked, confused.

"Yes, a complete, total, epic fail," Jada said, sitting up in the chair and swinging her feet to dangle off the side of the chaise. "Each semester on the first day of class I do an informal assessment of the students. I threw out a few basic ballet terms for them to do the move. Well, let's just say, some were in first position when they should have been in fourth position. Many were in second position when they should have been in first. When I said releve, some did a plie. It was horrendous."

"What are you going to do?"

"There may be a lot of failing grades if they don't get their act together," Jada said, leaning back on the chaise. "How was your first class?"

"It was good," Estelle said reflectively.

"Good to hear," Jada said.

"About yesterday," Estelle said leaning back in the recliner in Jada's office. "But, before I go any further, I have to say that your office is more comfortable than mine. I wouldn't be able to get any work done in here. It's relaxing like a needed retreat."

"I'm going to let you in on a little secret. I purposely made sure I designed my office space with comfort and relaxation in mind. At one time in my life, this here office was the only place I could be in and have peace," Jada said, closing her eyes. "I spent many nights here. When I didn't want to face my world outside of work, I would get dinner from the food court and return to my office."

"I certainly know that has changed for you," Estelle said. "The words you spoke yesterday certainly show you find your peace in God now."

"Yes, I do."

"Thank you for taking me to the river. It's what I needed. It really helped me."

"I'm glad," Jada said. "I'm also hungry."

Smiling, Estelle said, "I'm going to gain weight hanging around your pregnant behind."

"No one says you have to eat every time I eat. You choose to," Jada said smiling.

"I don't eat every time you eat," Estelle said. "You're still a mess. But, I actually am hungry, too."

"Then let's go eat," Jada said, pushing herself up from the chaise.

"Yeah, what the pregnant lady said," Estelle said, laughing.

"Oh, you got jokes," Jada said sarcastically as she locked her office door. "Corny ones."

"Yeah, yeah," Estelle said, still laughing as the two walked out of the door of the building where her office was housed.

"I can remember my first day as a freshman," Jada said looking around at the students who flowed through the streets of the city campus.

"You can remember that far back?" Estelle asked, laughing again.

"I see you still have jokes," Jada said with a smirk on her face. "You and I both know that you are the elder among us. But, yes, I can remember."

"I can't remember my first day of freshman year."

"That's what old age does to you," Jada said, laughing hysterically.

Shaking her head back and forth while smiling, Estelle said, "You were just waiting to get that in. Weren't you?"

"Yes," Jada said. "Yes, I was.

"You got me," Estelle said.

Placing emphasis on every word, Jada said, "Yes. I. Did."

"What are we going to eat?"

"I want a slice of pizza and a salad," Jada said.

"I'll get the same. Do you want to eat on campus or go to one of the pizzerias in the city?"

"Let's stay on campus. I don't feel like doing any extra walking. I'm tired today," Jada said, touching her belly.

"Fine with me," Estelle said. "We get more for our money eating on campus."

"I know that's right," Jada said as they neared the food court. "I hope it's not crowded in there today."

"We shall see," Estelle said.

"Yes, we shall," Jada said.

"Are you my echo?" Estelle asked jokingly.

Looking at Estelle and stating matter of factly, trying to keep a straight face, Jada said, "If I was your echo, Estelle, my words would have come back to you the same way you said them. That's what an echo does."

"Jada, you need to be quiet," Estelle said, laughing. "You know you want to smile."

Bursting into laughter, Jada said, "I don't know why I'm so silly today."

"I don't know either, but it's what I need," Estelle said as they stepped out of the elevator into the food court. "Looks like there's a crowd."

Sitting down in the middle of the food court, Jada said, "Although it's crowded in here at least it didn't take long to get through the line."

"No, it didn't," Estelle agreed, placing her straw in the disposable cup. "Thank goodness."

"Yes, thank goodness. I don't know how much longer I could have waited to eat. I am so hungry," Jada said, taking a bite of her pepperoni pizza. "This tastes so great."

Smiling, Estelle observed the hustle and bustle of the student body in the food court and said, "I can always pick the freshmen out of the crowd. They stick out like sore thumbs. They're the ones who look like they don't know where to go, can't figure out what to choose to eat for lunch and are seeking out a face they know. Maybe someone they sat next to in one of their classes. When no one is found, they find a table situated off by itself and sit and eat alone."

"Or they're like I was on my first day of college," Jada said, sipping her ice water.

"And may I ask, how were you on your first day of college?"

"For one thing, I didn't stick out like a sore thumb," Jada said, setting her pizza on her plate. "But that was only because I attended a college an older cousin of mine also attended. During my senior year of high school and her sophomore year of college, I would visit her often on weekends. I got to know people. I made friends. I knew exactly where to eat. I always found a familiar face in the crowd."

"Good for you," Estelle said. "Many aren't fortunate to have such a smooth transition. I surely didn't."

"Were you the student who found a table situated off by itself and ate alone?"

"Yes, that was me. It was awful!"

"You survived," Jada said, eating a forkful of salad.

"Geez, a little sympathy," Estelle said, rolling her eyes and shaking her head jokingly.

"Sympathy?" Jada asked and chuckled. "Yeah, okay."

Smiling at her friend, Estelle said, "I think I may have found a nice home to rent."

"That's good," Jada said, eating another forkful of salad. "How many rooms?"

"Five," Estelle said after chewing a bite of cheese pizza. "It's a one-bedroom, one-bathroom house with a living room, dining room and kitchen. It's a small house, but small is fine until I find the right house I want to buy."

"One floor or two floors?"

"One."

"Nice," Jada said.

"The landlord is willing to allow me to live there on a month-to-month lease, in the event that I find a house to buy within the year so I can move out easily."

"That sure is nice. Most landlords are not letting you move in without signing a one-year lease agreement. Are you going to choose that house?"

"Yes," Estelle said confidently.

"I know you're happy to have your house sold. I'm happy for you," Jada said, looking at Estelle. "I really am happy for you."

"Thank you," Estelle said. "It's been a journey."

"A journey that you walked with grace."

CHAPTER TWENTY-FIVE

Lacing her running shoes, then stepping outside of Jada's apartment, Estelle took in the bright sunlight. She stood for a moment to bask in it. Closing her eyes and tilting her head back, the warmth of the summer sun felt good on her face.

"Summer, I'll miss you when you go," Estelle spoke quietly.

Before Estelle began to run, she did walking lunges. Next, she did a kneeling hip flexor stretch. The hip flexor stretch was followed by side stretches and hip circles. Estelle ended her stretching with a standing quad stretch. She was ready to run. The breeze felt great. The more momentum she gained, the heavier the wind pressed upon her face. It felt great. Estelle's morning runs were freeing and refreshing. She could have ninety nine problems, but when she was running, she didn't have one. Some people preferred toxic vices to ease their minds and remove their worries. For Estelle, running was the answer. No matter what was going on in her life, after God, she had running. As funny as it sounded, she told people that often. Running was her stress release.

Rounding the corner, Estelle ran right into a crowded street. Although her usual route, today a street fair was being held in Jada's neighborhood. Estelle had forgotten. She would have rerouted her usual route if she would have remembered. Slightly slowing her speed, she weaved in and out of people of different ages, colors and races. As she ran, the crowd became dense, making it more difficult to maneuver. Estelle's jog became a walk.

Slowing down, Estelle took in the sound of the African drums. As she walked, the sound became louder, fiercer and more powerful. She pressed her way through the crowd. Getting a good view, she saw an all-male ensemble playing the Djembe drums. The ensemble formed a circle and in the middle was a group of dancers engaging in traditional African dance. It was beautiful. Men and women were clothed in colorful, traditional, African garb. The drumming and the dancing was so inviting. Moving to the beat of the drums, Estelle watched as people on the outside of the circle moved freely inside of the circle to dance. Crowd participation was encouraged.

Swirling and swaying; bending and reaching, Estelle lost herself in the beating of the drums. Eyes closed, hands lifted to the sky, she arched her back up and down in a syncopated move to the beat. The sound vibrated within her as her chest pulsated in and out while her feet marched. At that moment, Estelle had another reassurance of peace. God lived within her. With that singular fact, she knew that all would be well. This time around, Estelle was choosing God. Along with that, she was choosing herself. Nothing was more freeing than to choose herself in a world so fixated on having a man. Not that it was etched in stone that she would never revisit the idea of being in a relationship, even marrying again, however for this season of her life, she was content with being single.

As the beat became more intense and faster, Estelle made her way out of the circle. Scanning the crowd, she saw all hues of brown. Vendors lined the streets, selling their handmade wares. There were T-shirts, dashikis, African drums, beaded necklaces, shell earrings, head wraps. Young girls and women were sitting in tents getting their hair braided, two to three pair of hands moving swiftly through manes of thick hair, creating beautiful braided styles. Older women of African descent were teaching younger women multiple ways to wear traditional head dress. Estelle waited patiently for her turn to have her head wrapped.

Sitting down on the ground, padded with handmade mats, the older woman with soft wrinkles around her eyes spoke quietly to Estelle.

"Today I will teach you how to wear a gele. It is a traditional Nigerian head tie. You may choose your head tie," the older woman said, gently placing Estelle's hands on top of colorful, beautiful pieces of fabric.

"This one," Estelle said, choosing a blue fabric and placing it in the woman's hands.

"Blue. Beautiful," the older woman said as she folded and gathered the cloth to begin wrapping the fabric around Estelle's head.

Gathering and folding, then gathering and folding some more, the older woman tied the gele, securing it. Handing Estelle a mirror, she said, "Beautiful."

Looking at herself in the mirror, Estelle smiled. It did look beautiful on her.

Estelle enjoyed the joyous atmosphere a little longer. She sampled a deep fried plantain dish called dodo. It was delicious. She also ate akara, deep fried bean cakes. She had had akara once before. They tasted as great as she had remembered. The morning turned to afternoon and Estelle decided to make her way back to Jada's apartment.

Starting out in a slow jog, Estelle slowly picked up her pace. The faster she ran, she could feel the pavement beneath her feet. Some of the ground was smooth. Some of it was rocky and uneven. Cracks in the sidewalk allowed for weeds to make their way up to see the light of day. Estelle ran through a section of the sidewalk, heavily populated with weeds. As she ran further and further, the beating of the drums could be heard faintly in the distance. The memory of the rhythmic beats pulsated in her heart. She felt alive. Getting her second wind and gaining more momentum, Estelle sprinted down a straightway part of the sidewalk. The more she ran, the sidewalk became less populated. It was open and clear of other people. She had the sidewalk to herself. Cars drove up and down the street, while she was the lone individual on the sidewalk. At that moment, she felt close to God. Maybe closer than she had ever felt before. She ran on the sidewalk alone, yet she wasn't alone. The more she thought about it, she was never alone. God had always been there. In her valleys, He was there. He lifted her up. When she lost her baby, God comforted her. When she had to forgive someone who wasn't sorry, God was her strength. When she felt like she couldn't go on, God was her hope.

When Estelle reached Jada's apartment, she went straight to the kitchen. She grabbed a bottled water out of the refrigerator, opened it and drank it as she leaned against the kitchen counter. She walked to the door to Jada's room, looked in to find her friend asleep. Estelle closed the door to Jada's bedroom and walked further down the hall to the second bedroom, which she used while staying at Jada's. Her belongings could now fit in one room. All of her material items had been condensed to one room. Sitting on the bed, she pulled a box close to her. Opening it, the first thing she laid her eyes on was her grandmother's teapot. Holding it for a few seconds, she sat it on the bed when she saw an ultrasound picture peeking out from beneath a book of hers. Picking it up, she sat and stared at the picture of her unborn baby. Her baby. She didn't feel sad. She was no longer angry. She would never know why her baby had to die, but she had made a decision to not put herself through the agony of the why me game for the rest of her life. She simply left it as an unanswered mystery and made peace with not knowing why.

Placing the ultrasound picture back in the box, she leaned back on the headboard. She knew she would be okay. God had gotten her through the worst time of her life. She trusted Him to get her through another day, another month, another year; the rest of her life. Estelle knew that there would be days ahead of her with situations that would still cause her pain. There would be times that would bring tears. But, she knew, she would just need to allow herself to cry a little and after she had cried, to keep it moving. Life was made for living and that's what she was going to do, live it.

THE END